Remember the Alamo!

Amelia E. Barr

A Beka Book® Pensacola, FL 32523-9100
a ministry of PENSACOLA CHRISTIAN COLLEGE

Other Historic Fiction Novels

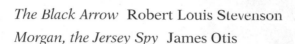

The Black Arrow Robert Louis Stevenson

Morgan, the Jersey Spy James Otis

Remember the Alamo! by Amelia E. Barr
originally published in 1888

Staff Credits
Editor: Brian Ashbaugh
Designer: John Halbach
Cover illustration by Jason Montgomery

A Beka Book, a Christian textbook ministry of Pensacola Christian College, is designed to
meet the need for Christian textbooks and teaching aids. The purpose of this publishing
ministry is to help Christian schools reach children and young people for the Lord and
train them in the Christian way of life.

Barr, Amelia Edith Huddleston, 1831–1919.
    Remember the Alamo! / Amelia E. Barr;
    editor, Brian Ashbaugh.
    iv, 256 p. ; 19 cm.
    Originally published in 1888.
    1. Alamo (San Antonio, Tex.)—Fiction;
2. Texas—History—Fiction. III. Ashbaugh, Brian S.
IV. A Beka Book, Inc.
Library of Congress: PS1072.B12 B45 2000
Dewey System: 813

Contents

chapter 1

The City in the Wilderness

*I*n A.D. 1692, a few Franciscan monks began to
build a city. The site chosen was a lovely wilderness hundreds of miles away from civilization on every side
and surrounded by savage and warlike tribes. But the spot
was as beautiful as the garden of God. It was shielded by
picturesque mountains, watered by two rivers, carpeted
with flowers innumerable, and shaded by trees joyful with
the notes of a multitude of singing birds. One of the rivers
was fed by a hundred springs. The monks called it the San
Antonio, and on its banks they built three noble missions.
Soon the shining white stone of the neighborhood rose in
graceful domes and spires above the trees.

Certainly these priests had to fight as well as to pray.
The Indians did not suffer them to take possession of their
Eden without passionate and practical protest. But what
the monks had taken, they kept, and the fort and the
soldier followed the priest and the Cross. Before long, the
beautiful mission became a beautiful city, about which a
sort of fame full of romance and mystery gathered.

Sanguine French traders ventured there with fancy
wares from New Orleans, and Spanish dons[2] from the

---

[1]dons—gentlemen; men of rank

wealthy cities of Central Mexico, and from the splendid
homes of Chihuahua, came there to buy. And from the
villages of Connecticut, and the woods of Tennessee, and
the lagoons of Mississippi, adventurous Americans
entered the Texan territory at Nacogdoches. They went
through the land, buying horses and lending their ready
rifles and stout hearts to every effort of that constantly
increasing body of Texans, who, even in their swaddling
bands, had begun to cry *Freedom!*

At length this cry became a clamor that shook even
the old viceroyal palace in Mexico. In San Antonio it
gave a certain pitch to all conversation, and made men
wear their cloaks and display their arms with that de-
monstrative air of independence they called *los
Americano*. For, though the Americans were numerically
few, they were like the pinch of salt in a pottage—they
gave the snap and savor to the whole community.

Over this Franciscan-Moorish city the sun set in a
haze of saffron, amethyst, and opal one evening in May
1835. The white, flat-roofed, terraced houses—each one
in its flowery court—and the domes and spires of the
missions, with their gilded crosses, had a miragelike
beauty in the rare, soft atmosphere, as if a dream of Old
Spain had been materialized in a wilderness of the New
World.

On this evening, as the hour of the Angelus[2] approached, the narrow streets and the great squares were
crowded with a mosaic of humanity that assaulted and
captured the senses at once. A tall, sinewy American

---

[2]Angelus—call to prayer

with a rifle across his shoulder was paying some money to a Mexican in blue velvet and red silk, whose breast was covered with little silver images of his favorite saints. A party of Mexican officers were strolling to the Alamo; some in white linen and scarlet sashes, others glittering with color and golden ornaments. Side by side with these were monks of various orders: the Franciscan in his blue gown and large white hat; the Capuchin in his brown serge; the Brother of Mercy in his white flowing robes. Add to these diversities Indian peasants in ancient sandals; women dressed as in the days of Cortez and Pizarro; Mexican vendors of every kind; Jewish traders; rancheros[3] astride fine horses; Apache and Comanche braves on spying expeditions; and, in this various crowd, yet by no means of it, small groups of Americans, watchful, silent, armed to the teeth—and the mind may catch a glimpse of what the streets of San Antonio were in the year of our Lord 1835.

It was just before sunset that the city was always at its gayest point. Yet, at the first toll of the Angelus, a silence like that of enchantment fell upon it. As a mother cries hush to a noisy child, so the angel of the city seemed in this evening bell to bespeak a minute for holy thought. It was only a minute, for with the last note there was even an access of tumult. The doors and windows of the better houses were thrown open, ladies began to appear on the balconies, and there was a sound of laughter and merry greetings in every direction.

---

[3]rancheros [răn·chär′ōs]—ranchers

Yet, amid this sunset glamour of splendid color, of velvet, silk, and gold embroidery, the man who would have certainly first attracted a stranger's eye wore the plain costume common in that day to all American gentlemen—only black cloth and white linen and a row palmetto hat with a black ribbon around it. He wore his simple garments with the air of a man having authority, and he returned the continual salutations of rich and poor as one who had been long familiar with public appreciation.

It was Dr. Robert Worth, a physician whose fame had penetrated to the utmost boundaries of the territories of New Spain. He had been twenty-seven years in San Antonio. He was a familiar friend in every home. In sickness and in death he had come close to the hearts in them. Protected at first by the powerful Urrea family, he had found it easy to retain his nationality, and yet live down envy and suspicion. The rich had shown him their gratitude with gold, the poor he had never sent unrelieved away, and they had all given him their love.

When in the second year of his residence he married Doña[4] Maria Flores, he gave, even to doubtful officials, security for his political intentions. And his future conduct had seemed to warrant their fullest confidence. In those never ceasing American invasions between 1803 and 1832, he had been the friend and succourer of his countrymen, but never their confederate; their adviser, but never their confidant.

_____

[4]Doña [dō′nyä]—Spanish courtesy title for a lady

He was a tall, muscular man of a distinguished appearance. His hair was white. His face was handsome and good to see. He was a man of few words, but his eyes were closely observant of all within their range, and they asked searching questions. He had a reverent soul, wisely tolerant as to creeds, and he loved his country with a passion which absence from it only intensified. He was believed to be a thoroughly practical man, fond of accumulating land and gold; but his daughter Antonia knew that he had in reality a noble imagination. When he spoke to her of the woods, she felt the echoes of the forest ring through the room; when of the sea, the walls melted away in a horizon of long, rolling waves.

He was thinking of Antonia as he walked slowly to his home in the suburbs of the city. Of all his children she was the nearest to him. She had his mother's beauty. She had also his mother's upright rectitude of nature. The Iberian[5] strain had passed her absolutely by. She was a northern rose in a tropical garden. As he drew near to his own gates, he involuntarily quickened his steps. He knew that Antonia would be waiting. He could see among the thick flowering shrubs her tall, slim figure clothed in white. As she came swiftly down the dim aisles to meet him, he thought of her. Antonia concentrated in herself his memory of home, mother, and country. As he entered the garden, his smile answered her smile and she slipped her hand into his. There was no need for any words of salutation.

---

[5]Iberian—of Spain

The full moon had risen. The white house stood clearly out in its radiance. The lattices were wide open and the parlor lighted. They walked slowly toward it, between hedges of white camelias and scarlet japonicas. Vanilla, patchuli, verbena, wild wandering honeysuckle—a hundred other scents—perfumed the light, warm air. As they came near the house there was a sound of music, soft and tinkling, with a rhythmic accent as pulsating as a beating heart.

"It is Don Luis, father."

"Ah! He plays well—and he looks well."

They had advanced to where Luis was distinctly visible. He was within the room, but leaning against the open door, playing upon a mandolin. Robert Worth smiled as he offered his hand to him. Young Don Luis Alveda had all the romance of the past in his name, his home, and his picturesque costume, and all the enchantments of hope and enthusiasm in his handsome face.

"Luis, I am glad to see you. I felt your music as soon as I heard it."

He was glancing inquiringly around the room as he spoke, and Antonia answered the look:

"Mother and Isabel are supping with Doña Valdez. There is to be a dance. I am waiting for you, Father. You must put on your velvet vest."

"And you, Luis?"

"I do not go. I asked the judge for the appointment, and he refused me. Very well! I care not to drink chocolate and dance in his house. One hand washes the other, and one cousin should help another."

"Why did he refuse you?"

"Who can tell?" Luis shrugged his shoulders expressively, and added, "He gave the office to Blas-Sangre."

"Ah!"

"Yes, it is so—naturally. Blas-Sangre is rich, and when the devil of money condescends to appear, every little devil rises up to do him homage."

"Let it pass, Luis. Suppose you come with us, and show those dandy soldiers from the Alamo how to dance."

"Pardon! I have not yet ceased to cross myself at the affront of this morning. And the Señora Valdez is in the same mind as her husband. I should be received by her like a dog at mass. I am going tomorrow to the American colony on the Colorado."

"Be careful, Luis. These Austin colonists are giving great trouble—there have been whispers of very strong measures. I speak as a friend."

"My heart to yours! But let me tell you this about the Americans—their drum is in the hands of one who knows how to beat it."

"As a matter of hearsay, are you aware that three detachments of troops are on their way from Mexico?"

"For Texas?"

"For Texas."

"What are three detachments? Can a few thousand men put Texas under lock and key? I assure you not, Señor; but now I must say adieu!"

He took the doctor's hand, and, as he held it, turned his luminous face and splendid eyes upon Antonia. A sympathetic smile brightened her own face like a flame. Then he went silently away, and Antonia watched him disappear among the shrubbery.

"Come, Antonia! I am ready. We must not keep the Señora waiting too long."

"I am ready, father." Her voice was almost sad, and yet it had a tone of annoyance in it. "Don Luis is so imprudent," she said. "He is always in trouble. He is full of enthusiasms; he is as impossible as his favorite, Don Quixote."[6]

"And I thank God, Antonia, that I can yet feel with him. Woe to the centuries without Quixotes! Nothing will remain to them but—Sancho Panzas."[7]

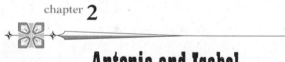

chapter 2

Antonia and Isabel

For many years there had never been any doubt in the mind of Robert Worth as to the ultimate destiny of Texas, though he was by no means an adventurer and had come into the beautiful land by a sequence of natural and businesslike events. He was born in New

---

[6]Don Quixote—The idealistic hero of Miguel de Cervantes's novel, *Don Quixote*.

[7]Sancho Panza—Quixote's peasant squire who, unlike his master, has no ambition.

York. In that city he studied his profession and, in 1803, began its practice in an office near Contoit's Hotel, opposite the City Park. One day he was summoned there to attend a sick man. His patient proved to be Don Jaime Urrea, and the rich Mexican grandee[8] conceived a warm friendship for the young physician.

At that time, France had just ceded to the United States the territory of Louisiana, and its western boundary was a subject about which Americans were then angrily disputing. They asserted that it was the Rio Grande, but Spain, who naturally did not want Americans so near her own territory, denied the claim and made the Sabine River[9] the dividing line. And as Spain had been the original possessor of Louisiana, she considered herself authority on the subject.

The question was on every tongue, and it was but natural that it should be discussed by Urrea and his physician. In fact, they talked continually of the disputed boundary, and of Mexico. Mexico was then a name to conjure by. She was as yet a part of Spain and shared in all her ancient glories. She was a land of romance, and her very name tasted on the lips of gold, and of silver, and of precious stones. Urrea easily persuaded the young man to return to Mexico with him.

The following year there was a suspicious number of American visitors and traders in San Antonio, and one of the Urreas was sent with a considerable number of troops to garrison the city. For Spain was well aware that,

---

[8]grandee—nobleman
[9]Sabine River—present-day boundary between Texas and Louisiana

however statesmen might settle the question, the young
and adventurous of the American people considered
Texas United States territory and would be well inclined
to take possession of it by force of arms if an opportunity offered.

Robert Worth accompanied General Urrea to San
Antonio, and the visit was decisive as to his future life.
The country enchanted him. He was smitten with love
for it, as men are smitten with a beautiful face. The
white Moorish city had one special charm for him—it
was seldom quite free from Americans. Among the
medieval loungers in the narrow streets, it filled his heart
with joy to see at intervals two or three big men in
buckskin or homespun.[10]

His inclination to remain in San Antonio was settled
by his marriage. Doña Maria Flores, though connected
with the great Mexican families of Yturbide and
Landesa, owned much property in San Antonio. She
had been born within its limits and educated in its
convent, and a visit to Mexico and New Orleans had
only strengthened her attachment to her own city. She
was a very pretty woman, with an affectionate nature,
but she was not intellectual. Even in the convent the
sisters had not considered her clever.

But Robert Worth had never regretted that his
Maria did not play on the piano, and paint on velvet,
and work fine embroideries for the altars. They had
passed nearly twenty-six years together in more than
ordinary content and prosperity. Yet no life is without

---

[10]homespun—a coarse cloth made by pioneers

cares and contentions, and Robert Worth had had to face circumstances several times which had brought the real man to the front.

The education of his children had been such a crisis. He had two sons and two daughters, and for them he anticipated a wider and grander career than he had chosen for himself. When his eldest child, Thomas, had reached the age of fourteen, he determined to send him to New York. He spoke to Doña Maria of this intention, describing Columbia[11] to her with all the affectionate pride of a student for his alma mater. The boy's grandmother also still lived in the home wherein he himself had grown to manhood. His eyes filled with tears when he remembered the red brick house on Canal Street, with its white door and dormer windows, and its one cherry tree in the strip of garden behind.

But Doña Maria's national and religious principles, or rather prejudices, were very strong. She regarded the college of San Juan de Lateran in Mexico as the fountainhead of knowledge. Her confessor had told her so. All the Yturbides and Landesas had graduated at San Juan.

But the resolute father would have none of San Juan. "I know all about it, Maria," he said. "They will teach Thomas Latin very thoroughly. They will make him proficient in theology[12] and metaphysics.[13] They will let him dabble in algebra and Spanish literature,

---

[11]Columbia College, in New York City; now Columbia University
[12]theology—here referring to Catholic doctrine
[13]metaphysics—philosophy

and with great pomp, they will give him his degree, and
'the power of interpreting Aristotle all over the world.'
What kind of an education is that for a man who may
have to fight the battles of life in this century?"

And since the father carried his point it is immaterial
what precise methods he used. Two years afterward,
Antonia followed her brother to New York, and this time,
the mother made less opposition. Perhaps she divined
that opposition would have been still more useless than in
the case of the boy. For Robert Worth had one invincible
determination: it was, that this beautiful child, who so
much resembled a mother whom he idolized, should be,
during the most susceptible years of her life, under that
mother's influence.

He was well repaid for the self-denial her absence
entailed when Antonia came back to him, alert, self-
reliant, and industrious—an intelligent and responsive
companion. Also a neat and capable housekeeper, she
gave to his home that American air it lacked and set upon
his table the well-cooked meats and delicate dishes which
he had often longed for.

John, the youngest boy, was still in New York finishing
his course of study, but regarding Isabel, there seemed to be
a tacit relinquishment of the purpose so inflexibly carried
out with her brothers and sister. Isabel was entirely different from them. Her father had watched her carefully, and
come to the conviction that it would be impossible to make
her nature take the American mintage. She was as distinctly Iberian as Antonia was Anglo-American.

In her brothers the admixture of races had been only
as alloy to metal. Thomas Worth was but a darker copy of

his father. John had the romance and sensitive honor of old Spain, mingled with the love of liberty and the practical temper of those Worths who had defied both Charles the First and George the Third. But Isabel had no soul-kinship with her father's people. Robert Worth had seen in the Yturbide residencia in Mexico the family portraits which they had brought with them from Castile. Isabel was the Yturbide of her day. She had all their physical traits, and from her large golden-black eyes the same passionate soul looked forth. He felt that it would be utter cruelty to send her among people who must always be strangers to her.

So Isabel dreamed away her childhood at her mother's side, or with the sisters in the convent, learning from them such simple and useless matters as they considered necessary for a damosel[14] of family and fortune. On the night of the Señora Valdez's reception, she had astonished everyone by the adorable grace of her dancing, and the captivating way in which she used her fan. Her fingers touched the guitar as if they had played it for a thousand years. She sang a Spanish romancero of El mio Cid[15] with all the fire and tenderness of a Castilian maid.

Her father watched her with troubled eyes. He almost felt as if he had no part in her. The thought gave him an unusual anxiety, for he knew this night that the days were fast approaching which would test to extremity the affection which bound his family together. He contrived to draw Antonia aside for a few moments.

---

[14]damosel—a young woman
[15]El mio Cid—a legendary Spanish hero

"Is she not wonderful?" he asked. But Antonia read the concern in his eyes.

"Father, are you troubled? What is it? Not Isabel, surely?"

"Not Isabel, primarily. Antonia, I have been expecting something for twenty years. It is coming."

"And you are sorry?"

"I am anxious, that is all. Go back to the dancers. In the morning we can talk."

In the morning the doctor was called very early by someone needing his skill. Antonia heard the swift footsteps and eager voices, and watched him ride away with the messenger. The incident in itself was a usual one, but she was conscious that her soul was moving uneasily and questioningly in some new and uncertain atmosphere.

She had felt it on her first entrance into Señora Valdez's gran sala[16]—a something irrepressible in the faces of all the men present. She remembered that even the servants had been excited, and that they stood in small groups, talking with suppressed passion and with much demonstrativeness. And the officers from the Alamo! How conscious they had been of their own importance! What airs of condescension and of an almost insufferable protection they had assumed! Now that she recalled the faces of Judge Valdez and other men of years and position, she understood that there had been in them something out of tone with the occasion. In the atmosphere of the fiesta she had only felt it.

---

[16]gran sala—great room or reception hall; parlor

In the solitude of her room, she could apprehend its
nature.

For she had been born during those stormy days
when Magee and Bernardo, with twelve hundred Americans, first flung the banner of Texan independence to the
wind; when the fall of Nacogdoches sent a thrill of
sympathy through the United States, and enabled Cos
and Toledo, and the other revolutionary generals in
Mexico, to carry their arms against Old Spain to the very
doors of the viceroyal palace. She had heard from her
father many a time the whole brave, brilliant story—the
same story which has been made in all ages from the
beginning of time. Only the week before, they had talked
it over as they sat under the great fig-tree together.

"History but repeats itself," the doctor had said then,
"for when the Mexicans drove the Spaniards, with their
court ceremonies, their monopolies and taxes, back to
Spain, they were just doing what the American colonists
did when they drove the English royalists back to England. It was natural, too, that the Americans should help
the Mexicans, for at first they were but a little band of
patriots. The American-Saxon has, like the Anglo-Saxon,
an irresistible impulse to help the weaker side. Oh,
Antonia! The cry of Freedom! Who that has a soul can
resist it?"

She remembered this conversation as she stood in
the pallid dawning and watched her father ride swiftly
away. The story of the long struggle in all its salient
features flashed through her mind, and she understood
that it is not the sword alone that gives liberty. There
must be patience before courage; great ideas must

germinate for years in the hearts of men before the sword can reap the harvest.

With an impulse natural, but neither analyzed nor understood, she lifted her prayer-book and began to recite "the rising prayer." As she knelt, up rose the sun, flooding her white figure and her fair unbound hair with the radiance of the early morning. The matin bells chimed from the convent and the churches, and the singing birds began to flutter their bright wings and praise God also, "in their Latin."

She took her breakfast alone. The Señora never came downstairs so early. Isabel had wavering inclinations, and generally followed them. Sometimes, even her father had his cup of strong coffee alone in his study. So the first meal of the day was usually, as perhaps it ought to be, a selfishly silent one. "Too much enthusiasm and chattering at breakfast are like too much red at sunrise," the doctor always said. "A dull, bad day follows it."

In the Señora's room, the precept was either denied or defied. Antonia heard the laughter and conversation through the closed door and easily divined the subject of it. It was but natural. The child had a triumph, one that appealed strongly to her mother's pride and predilections. It was a pleasant sight to see them in the shaded sunshine exulting themselves happily in it.

The Señora, plump and still pretty, reclined upon a large gilded bed. Its splendid silk coverlet and pillows cased in embroidery and lace made an effective background for her. She leaned with a luxurious indolence among them, sipping chocolate. Isabel was on a couch

of the same description. She wore a satin petticoat and a
loose linen waist richly trimmed with lace. Her hands
were folded above her head, and her tiny feet, shod in
satin, were quivering like a bird's wings, as if they were
keeping time with the restlessness of her spirit.

She had large eyes, dark and bright; strong eyebrows,
a pale complexion with a flood of brilliant color in the
cheeks, dazzling even teeth, and a small, handsome
mouth. Her black hair, loose and flowing, caressed her
cheeks and temples in numberless little curls and ten-
drils. She had a look half-earnest and half-childlike, and
altogether charming. Antonia adored her, and she was
pleased to listen to the child, telling over again the pretty
things that had been said to her.

"Only Don Luis was not there at all, Antonia. There
is always something wanting."

The Señora looked sharply at her. "Don Luis was not
desirable. He was better away—much better!"

"But why?"

"Because, Antonia, he is suspected. There is an
American called Houston. Don Luis met him in
Nacogdoches. He has given his soul to him, I think. He
would have fought Morello about him, if the captain
could have drawn his sword in such a quarrel. I should
not have known about the affair had not Señora Valdez
told me. Your father says nothing against the Americans."

"Perhaps, then, he knows nothing against them."

"You will excuse me, Antonia; not only the living but
the dead must have heard of their wickedness. They are
a nation of ingrates. Ingrates are cowards. It was these
words Captain Morello said, when Don Luis drew his

sword, made a circle with its point and stood it upright
in the center. It was a challenge to the whole garrison,
and about this fellow Houston, whom he calls his
friend!"

"It is easier to talk than to fight. Morello's tongue is
sharper than his sword."

"Captain Morello was placing his sword beside that
of Don Luis when the Commandant interfered. He would
not permit his officers to fight in such a quarrel. Just
reflect upon the folly of a boy like Don Luis, challenging
a soldier like Morello!"

"He was in no danger, mother," said Antonia scornfully.
"Morello is a bully, who wears the pavement out with his
spurs and sabre. His weapons are for show. Americans,
at least, wear their arms for use, and not for ornament."

"Listen, Antonia! I will not have them spoken of.
They are infidels, all of them! The bishop, when he was
here last confirmation, told me so."

"Mother!"

"At least they are unbaptized Christians, Antonia. If
you are not baptized, the devil sends you to do his work.
As for Don Luis, he is a very Judas! Ah, Maria Santissima!
How I do pity his good mother!"

"Poor Don Luis!" said Isabel plaintively. "He is so
handsome, and he sings like a very angel. And he loves
my father; he wanted to be a doctor, so that he could
always be with him. Let us talk no more about the
Americans. I am weary of them; as Tia Rachella says,
'they have their spoon in everyone's mess.' "

Antonia, whose heart was burning, only stooped
down and closed her sister's pretty mouth with a kiss.

Her tongue was impatient to speak for the father, and grandmother, and the friends so dear to her; but she possessed great discretion, and also a large share of that rarest of all womanly graces, the power under provocation of "putting on patience the noble."

chapter **3**

Sam Houston

*I*t is the fashion now to live for the present, but the men who builded the nation reverenced the past, and therefore they could work for the future. As Robert Worth rode through the streets of San Antonio that afternoon, he was thinking, not of his own life, but of his children's and of the generations which should come after them.

The city was flooded with sunshine and crowded with a pack-train going to Sonora. The animals were restlessly protesting against the heat and flies; their Mexican drivers were in the pulqueria,[17] spending their last peso with their compadres, or with the escort of soldiers which was to accompany them. Their lieutenant, a gorgeously clad officer with a very distinguished air, was

---

[17]pulqueria [pōōl·kä′rĭ·ə]—tavern

coming slowly down the street to join them. He bowed
and smiled pleasantly to the doctor as he passed him,
and then in a few moments the word of command and
the shouting of men and the clatter of hoofs invaded the
enchanted atmosphere like an insult.

But the tumult scarcely jarred the thoughts of the
doctor's mind. They had been altogether of war and
rumors of war. Every hour that subtile consciousness
of coming events, which makes whole communities at
times prescient, was becoming stronger.

After leaving the city there were only a few Mexican
huts on the shady road leading to his own house. All
within them were asleep; even the fighting cocks tied
outside were dozing on their perches. He was unusu-
ally weary. He had been riding since dawn, and his
heart had not been in sympathy with his body; it had
said no good cheer to it, whispered no word of courage
or promise.

All at once his physical endurance seemed exhausted, and he saw the white wall and arched gateway
of his garden and the turrets of his home with an
inexpressible relief. But it was the hour of siesta, and
he was always careful not to let the requirements of his
profession disturb his household. So he rode quietly to
the rear, where he found a peasant nodding within the
stable door. He opened his eyes unnaturally wide, and
rose to serve his master.

"See you rub the mare down well, and give her corn
and water."

"To be sure, Señor, that is to be done. A stranger
has been here to-day—an American."

"What did he say to you?"

"That he would call again, Señor."

The incident was not an unusual one, and it did not trouble the doctor's mind. There was on the side of the house a low extension containing two rooms. These rooms belonged exclusively to him. One was his study, the place to which he went when he wanted to be alone with his own soul. There were a bed and bath and refreshments in the other room. He went directly to the latter and, after eating and washing, fell into a profound sleep.

At the hour before Angelus the house was as noisy and busy as if it had been an inn. The servants were running hither and thither, all of them expressing themselves in voluble Spanish. The cooks were quarrelling in the kitchen. Antonia was showing the table men, as she had to do afresh every day, how to lay the cloth and serve the dishes in the American fashion. When the duty was completed, she went into the garden to listen for the Angelus. She wore a simple, white muslin frock, with a straight skirt and low waist and short, full sleeves. It was confined by a blue belt with a gold buckle, and her feet were in sandalled slippers of black satin.

The Angelus tolled, and the thousands of "Hail Maries!" which blended with its swinging vibrations were uttered and left to their fate, as all spoken words must be. It lent for a moment a solemn beauty to the evening atmosphere. She was about to re-enter the house when she saw a stranger approaching it. He was dressed in a handsome buckskin suit and a wide Mexican hat, but

she knew at once that he was an American, and she
waited to receive him.

As soon as he saw her, he removed his hat and approached with it in his hand. He was a very tall, well
proportioned man, and his address had the grace and
polish of a cultured gentleman.

"I wish to see Dr. Worth, Doña."

With a gentle inclination of the head, she led him to
the door of her father's office. She was the only one in
the Doctor's family at all familiar with the room. The
Señora said so many books made her feel as if she were
in a church or monastery; she was afraid to say anything
but paternosters[18] in it. Isabel cowered before the poor
skeleton in the corner and at the centipedes and snakes
that filled the bottles on the shelves. There was not a
servant that would enter the room.

But Antonia did not regard books as a part of some
vague spiritual power. She knew the history of the
skeleton. She had seen the death of many of those "little
devils" corked up in alcohol. She knew that at this hour,
if her father were at home, he was always disengaged,
and she opened the door fearlessly, saying, "Father, here
is a gentleman who wishes to see you."

The doctor had refreshed himself, and, in a house-suit
of clean, white linen, was lying on a couch reading. He
arose with alacrity, and with his pleasant smile seemed to
welcome the intruder as he stepped behind him and
closed the door. Antonia had disappeared, leaving the
men alone.

---

[18]paternosters—recited prayers

"You are Doctor Robert Worth, sir?"

"And you are Sam Houston?"

The questions were answered in a hand grip and a sympathetic smile on both faces—the freemasonry of kindred spirits.

"I have a letter from your son Thomas, doctor, and I think, also, that you will have something to say to me, and I to you."

The most prudent of patriots could not have resisted this man. He had that true imperial look which all born rulers of men possess—that look that half coerces and wholly persuades. Robert Worth acknowledged its power by his instant and decisive answer.

"I have, indeed, much to say to you. We shall have dinner directly, then you will give the night to me?"

After a short conversation he led him into the sala and introduced him to Antonia. He himself had to prepare the Señora for her visitor, and he had a little quaking of the heart as he entered her room. She was dressed for dinner, and turned with a laughing face to meet him.

"I have been listening to the cooks quarrelling over the olla,[19] Roberto. But what can my poor Manuel say when your Irish woman attacks him. Listen to her! 'Take your dirty stew aff the fire then! Shure it isn't fit for a Christian to ate atall!' "

"I hope it is, Maria, for we have a visitor to-night."

"Who, then, my love?"

"Mr. Houston."

---

[19]olla—a stew of meat and vegetables

"Sam Houston? I will not see the man."

"I think you will, Maria. He has brought this letter for you from our son Thomas, and he has been so kind as to take charge of some fine horses and sell them well for him in San Antonio. When a man does us a kindness, we should say thank you."

"That is truth, if the man is not the Evil One. As for this Sam Houston, you should have heard what was said of him at the Valdez's."

"I did hear. Everything was a lie."

"But he is a very common man."

"Maria, do you call a soldier, a lawyer, a member of the United States Congress, a governor of a great State like Tennessee, a common man? Houston has been all of these things."

"But he—" The doctor hushed her with a gentle look, and took her hands in his own.

"Come down and smile upon him, Maria. I should like him to see a high-born Mexican lady. Are they not the kindest and fairest among all God's women? I know, at least, Maria, that you are kind and fair."

What good wife can resist her husband's wooing? Maria did not. She lifted her smiling face and whispered: "My Robert, it is a joy to please you. I will be kind; I will be grateful about Thomas. You shall see that I will make a pleasant evening."

So the triumphant husband went down, proud and happy, with his smiling wife upon his arm. Isabel was already in the room. She also wore a white frock, but her hair was pinned back with gold butterflies, and she had a beautiful golden necklace around her throat. The

Señora kept her word. She paid her guest great attention. She talked to him of his adventures with the
Indians. She requested her daughters to sing to him.
She told him stories of the old Castilian families with
which she was connected, and described her visit to
New Orleans with a great deal of pleasant humor. She
felt that she was doing herself justice—that she was
charming—and, consequently, she also was charmed
with the guest and the occasion which had been so
favorable to her.

After the ladies had retired, the doctor led his visitor
into his study. He sat down silently and placed a chair
for Houston. Both men hesitated for a moment to open
the conversation. Worth, because he was treading on
unknown ground; Houston, because he did not wish to
force, even by a question, a resolution which he felt sure
would come voluntarily.

Worth laid a letter upon the table, and said: "I
understand from this, that my son Thomas thinks the
time has come for decisive action."

"He is right. With such men as your son the founda-
tion of the state must be laid."

"I am glad Thomas has taken the position he has;
but you must remember, sir, that he is unmarried and
unembarrassed by many circumstances which render
decisive movement on my part a much more difficult
thing. Yet no man now living has watched the Ameri-
canizing of Texas with the interest that I have."

"You have been long on the watch, sir."

"I was here when my countrymen came first, in little
companies of five or ten men. I saw the party of twenty,

who joined the priest Hidalgo in 1810, when Mexico
made her first attempt to throw off the Spanish yoke."

"An unsuccessful attempt."

"Yes. The next year I made a pretended professional
journey to Chihuahua, to try and save their lives. I
failed. They were shot with Hidalgo there."

"Yet the strife for liberty went on."

"It did. Two years afterwards, Magee and Bernardo,
with twelve hundred Americans, raised the standard of
independence on the Trinity River. I saw them take this
very city, though it was ably defended by Salcedo. They
fought like heroes. I had many of the wounded in my
house. I succored them with my purse.

"It was a great deed for a handful of men."

"The fame of it brought young Americans by hundreds here. To a man they joined the Mexican party
struggling to free themselves from the tyranny of old
Spain. I do not think any one of them received money.
The love of freedom and the love of adventure were alike
their motive and their reward."

"Mexico owes these men a debt she has forgotten."

"She forgot it very quickly. In the following year,
though they had again defended San Antonio against the
Spaniards, the Mexicans drove all the Americans out of
the city their rifles had saved."

"You were here; tell me the true reason."

"It was not altogether ingratitude. It was the instinct
of self-preservation. The very bravery of the Americans
made the men whom they had defended hate and fear
them; and there was a continual influx of young men
from the States. The Mexicans said to each other:

'There is no end to these Americans. Very soon they will make a quarrel and turn their arms against us. They do not conform to our customs, and they will not take an order from any officer but their own.' "

Houston smiled. "What happened after this forcible expulsion of the American element from Texas?"

"Mexican independence was for a time abandoned, and the Spanish viceroys were more tyrannical than ever. But Americans still came, though they pursued different tactics. They bought land and settled on the great rivers. In 1821, Austin, with the permission of the Spanish viceroy in Mexico, introduced three hundred families."

"That was a step in the right direction."

"I do not need to tell you that Austin's colonists are a band of choice spirits, hardy working men, trained in the district schools of New England and New York— nearly every one of them a farmer or mechanic."

"They were the very material liberty needed. They have made homes."

"That is the truth. The fighters who preceded them owned nothing but their horses and their rifles. But these men brought with them their wives and their children, their civilization, their inborn love of freedom and their faith. They accepted the guarantee of the Spanish government, and they expected the Spanish government to keep its promises."

"It did not."

"It had no opportunity. The colonists were hardly settled when the standard of revolt against Spain was again raised. Santa Anna took the field for a republican form of government, and once more a body of Americans, under the Tennesseean, Long, joined the Mexican army."

"I remember that, well."

"In 1824, Santa Anna, Victoria, and Bravo drove the Spaniards forever from Mexico, and then they promulgated the famous constitution of 1824. It was a noble constitution, purely democratic and federal, and the Texan colonists to a man gladly swore to obey it. The form was altogether elective, and what particularly pleased the American element was the fact that the local government of every State was left to itself."

"I was sitting in the United States Congress when this constitution passed."

"I will not detain you with Mexican politics. It may be briefly said that for the last ten years there has been a constant fight between Pedraza, Guerrero, Bustamante, and Santa Anna for the Presidency of Mexico. After so much war and misery, the country is now ready to resign all the blessings the constitution of 1824 promised her. For peace she is willing to have a dictator in Santa Anna."

Houston's eyes flashed. "If Mexicans want a dictator let them bow down to Santa Anna! But do you think the 20,000 free-born Americans in Texas are going to have a dictator? They will have the constitution of 1824—or they will have independence, and make their own constitution! Yes, sir!"

"You know the men for whom you speak?"

"I have been up and down among them for two years. Just after I came to Texas I was elected to the convention which sent Stephen Austin to Mexico with a statement of our wrongs. Did we get any redress? No, sir! And as for poor Austin, is he not in the dungeons of the Inquisition? We have waited two years for an answer."

"Was this convention a body of any influence?"

"Influence! There were men there whose names will never be forgotten. They met in a log house—they wore buckskin and homespun—but I tell you, sir, they were debating the fate of unborn millions."

"Two years since Austin went to Mexico?"

"A two years' chapter of tyranny. In them Santa Anna has quite overthrown the republic of which we were a part. He has made himself dictator, and because our authorities have protested against the change they have been driven from office by a military force. I tell you, sir, the petty outrages everywhere perpetrated by petty officials have filled the cup of endurance. It is boiling over. Now, doctor, what are you going to do? Are you with us, or against us?"

"I have told you that I have been with my countrymen always—heart and soul with them."

The doctor spoke with some irritation, and Houston laid his closed hand hard upon the table to emphasize his reply:

"Heart and soul! Very good! But we want your body now. You must tuck your bowie-knife and your revolvers in your belt, and take your rifle in your hand, and be ready to help us drive the Mexican force out of this very city."

"When it comes to that I shall be no laggard."

But he was deathly pale, for he was suffering as men suffer who feel the sweet bonds of wife and children and home, and dread the rending of them apart. In a moment, however, the soul behind his white face made it visibly luminous. "Houston," he said, "whenever the cause of freedom needs me, I am ready. I shall want no second call. But is it not possible, that even yet—"

"It is impossible to avert what is already here. Within a few days, perhaps to-morrow, you will hear the publication of an edict from Santa Anna, ordering every American to give up his arms."

"What! Give up our arms! No! I will die fighting for mine, rather."

"Exactly. That is how every American in Texas feels about it. And if such a wonder as a coward exists among them, he understands that he may as well die fighting Mexicans, as die of hunger or be scalped by Indians. A large proportion of the colonists depend on their rifles for their daily food. All of them know that they must defend their own homes from the Comanche. Now, do you imagine that Americans will obey any such order? By all the great men of 1775, if they did, I would go over to the Mexicans and help them to wipe the degenerate cowards out of existence!"

He rose as he spoke; he looked like a flame, and his words cut like a sword. Worth caught fire at his vehemence and passion. He clasped his hands in sympathy as he walked with him to the door. They stood silently together for a moment on the threshold, gazing into the night. In the pale, mystical light of the full moon, the white city looked enchanted.

"It is a beautiful land," said the doctor.

"It is worthy of freedom," answered Houston. Then he went with long, swinging steps down the garden path and into the shadows beyond, and Worth turned in and closed the door.

He had been watching for this very hour for twenty years, and yet he found himself wholly unprepared for it. Like one led by confused and uncertain thoughts, he went about the room mechanically locking up his papers and the surgical instruments he valued so highly. As he did so he perceived the book he had been reading when Houston entered. It was lying open where he had laid it down. A singular smile flitted over his face. He lifted it and carried it closer to the light. It was his college Cicero.

"I was nineteen years old when I marked that passage," he said, "and I do not think I read it since, until tonight. I was reading it when Houston came into the room."

'But when thou considerest everything carefully and thoughtfully; of all societies none is of more importance, none more dear, than that which unites us with the commonwealth. Our parents, children, relations and neighbors are dear, but our fatherland embraces the whole round of these endearments. In its defence, who would not dare to die, if only he could assist it?'

chapter 4

The Edict

In the morning, Isabel took breakfast with her sister. This was always a pleasant event to Antonia. She petted Isabel, she waited upon her, sweetened her chocolate, spread her cakes with honey, and listened to all her complaints of Tia Rachela. Isabel came gliding in when Antonia was about half way through the meal. Her scarlet petticoat was gorgeous, her bodice white as snow, her hair glossy as a bird's wing, but her lips drooped and trembled, and there was the shadow of tears in her eyes.

"What has grieved you this morning, little dove?"

"It is Tia Rachela, as usual. The cross old woman! She is going to tell mi madre something. Antonia, you must make her keep her tongue between her teeth. I promised her to confess to Fray Ignatius, and she said I must also tell mi madre. I vowed to say twenty Hail Marias and ten Glorias, and she said 'I ought to go back to the convent.' "

"But what dreadful thing have you been doing, Iza?"

Iza blushed and looked into her chocolate cup, as she answered slowly: "I gave—a—flower—away. Only a suchil flower, Antonia, that—I—wore—last—night."

"Whom did you give it to, Iza?"

Iza hesitated, moved her chair close to Antonia, and then hid her face.

"But this is serious, darling. Surely you did not give it to Señor Houston?"

"Could you think I was so silly? When madre was talking to him last night, and when I was singing my pretty serenade, he heard nothing at all. He was thinking his own thoughts."

"Not to Señor Houston? Who then? Tell me, Iza."

"To—Don Luis."

"Don Luis! But he is not here. He went to the Colorado."

"How blind are you, Antonia! In New York they did not teach you to put this and that together. As soon as I saw Senor Houston, I said to myself: 'Don Luis was going to him—very likely they have met each other on the road—very likely Don Luis is back in San Antonio. He would not want to go away without bidding me good-by,' and, of course, I was right."

"But when did you see him last night? You never left the room."

"So many things are possible. My heart said to me when the talk was going on, 'Don Luis is waiting under the oleanders,' and I walked onto the balcony and there he was, and he looked so sad that I dropped my suchil flower to him, and Rachela saw me, for I think she has a million eyes—and that is the whole matter."

"But why did not Don Luis come in?"

"Mi madre forbade me to speak to him. That is the fault of the Valdez's."

"Then you disobeyed mi madre, and you know what Fray Ignatius and the Sisters have taught you about the fourth command."

"Oh, indeed, I did not think of the fourth command! Antonia, speak to Rachela, and make your little Iza happy. Fear is so bad for me. See, I do not even care for my cakes and honey this morning."

"I will give Rachela the blue silk kerchief I brought from New York. She will forget a great deal for that."

Antonia understood her sister's plight. She was not without experience herself. There was in New York a young American to whom her thoughts lovingly turned. She had promised to trust him and to wait for him, and neither silence nor distance had weakened her faith or her affection. Don Luis had also made her understand how hard it was to leave Isabel, just when he had hoped to woo and win her. He had asked Antonia to watch over his beloved, and to say a word in his favor when all others would be condemning him.

Her sympathy had been almost a promise, and, indeed, she thought Isabel could hardly have a more suitable lover. He was handsome, gallant, rich, and of good morals and noble family. They had been much together in their lives. Their childish affection had been permitted, and she felt quite sure that the parents of both had contemplated a stronger affection and a more lasting tie between them.

Antonia comprehended all without many words, but she took her sister into the garden, where they could be quite alone, and sought the girl's confidence there.

Isabel was ready enough to talk, and the morning was conducive to confidence. They strolled slowly between the myrtle hedges in the sweet gloom of over-shadowing trees, hearing only like a faint musical confusion the mingled murmur of the city.

"It was just here," said Isabel. "I was walking and sitting and doing nothing at all but looking at the trees and the birds and feeling happy, and Don Luis came to me. He might have come down from the skies, I was so astonished. And he looked so handsome, and he said such words! Oh, Antonia! they went straight to my heart."

"When was this, dear?"

"It was in the morning. I had been to mass with Rachela. I had said every prayer with my whole heart, and Rachela told me I might stay in the garden until the sun grew hot. And as soon as Rachela was gone, Don Luis came—came just as sudden as an angel."

"He must have followed you from mass."

"Perhaps."

"He should not have done that."

"Luis said he knew that it was decided that we should marry, but that he wanted me to be his wife because I loved him. I was too happy to speak."

"Oh, Iza!"

"Very well, Antonia! It is easy to say 'Oh, Iza'—but what would you have done?"

"Oh, my darling, I think you did nothing very wrong. Don't fret; I will take care of Rachela. Come, now, we must make a visit to our mother. She will be wondering at our delay."

The Señora had not yet risen. She had taken her chocolate, but was still drowsing. "I have had a bad night, children," she said, "full of dreadful dreams. It must have been that American. Yet, how handsome he is! And I assure you that he has the good manners of a courtier. Still, it was an imprudence, and Señora Valdez will make some great thing of it."

"You were in your own house, mother. What has Señora Valdez to do with the guest in it? We might as well make some great thing about Captain Morello being present at her party."

"I have to say to you, Antonia, that Morello is a Castilian. He has the parchments of his noble ancestry to show."

"And Señor Houston is an American—a Scotch-American, he said, last night. Pardon, my mother, but do you know what the men of Scotland are?"

"Si! They are monsters! Fray Ignatius has told me. They are heretics of the worst kind. It is their special delight to put to death good Catholic priests. I saw that in a book; it must be true."

"Oh, no, mother! It is not true! It is mere nonsense. Scotchmen do not molest priests, women, and children. They are the greatest fighters in the world."

"Quien sabe?[20] Who has taught you so much about these savages?"

"Indeed, mother, they are not savages. They are a very learned race of men, and very pious also. Jack has many Scotch-American friends. I know one of them very well—"

---

[20]Quien sabe? [kyĕn′ sä′bä]—Who knows?

"Jack knows many of them! That is likely. Your father would send him to New York. All kinds of men are in New York. Fray Ignatius says they have to keep an army of police there. No wonder! And my son is so full of nobilities, so generous, so honorable, he will not keep himself exclusive. He is the true resemblance of my brother Don Juan Flores. Juan was always pitying the poor and making friends with those beneath him. At last he went into the convent of the Bernardines and died like a very saint."

"I think our Jack will be more likely to die like a very hero. If there is any thing Jack hates, it is oppression. He would right a beggar, if he saw him wronged."

"Enough! I am tired of rights and wrongs. Let us talk a little about our dresses, for there will be a gay winter. Señora Valdez assured me of it; many soldiers are coming here, and we shall have parties, and cock-fights, and, perhaps, even a bull-feast."

"Oh!" cried Isabel clapping her hands enthusiastically, "a bull-feast! That is what I long to see!"

At this moment the doctor entered the room, and Isabel ran to meet him. No father could have resisted her pretty ways.

"What is making you so happy, queridita?"[21]

"Mi madre says there is perhaps to be a bull-feast this winter. Think of it! That is the one thing I long to see!"

With her clinging arms around him, and her eager face lifted to his for sympathy, the father could not dash

---

[21]queridita [kĕ′rä·dē′tə]—Little dear

the hope which he knew in his heart was very unlikely to be realized. Neither did he think it necessary to express opposition or disapproval for what had as yet no tangible existence. So he answered her with smiles and caresses, and a little quotation which committed him to nothing:

> "As, Panem et Circenses[22] was the cry
> Among the Roman populace of old;
> So, Pan y Toros![23] is the cry of Spain."

The Señora smiled appreciatively and put out her hand. "Pan y Toros!" she repeated. "And have you reflected, children, that no other nation in the world cries it. Only Spain and her children! That is because only men of the Spanish race are brave enough to fight bulls, and only Spanish bulls are brave enough to fight men."

She was quite pleased with herself for this speech, and finding no one inclined to dispute the statement, she went on to describe a festival of bulls she had attended in the city of Mexico. The subject delighted her, and she grew eloquent over it. Conscious only of Isabel's shining eyes and enthusiastic interest, she did not notice the air of thoughtfulness which had settled over her husband's face, nor yet Antonia's ill-disguised weariness and anxiety.

Later in the day, after the siesta, the Señora bid her daughters to call upon the American manteau-maker for her. The ride in the open carriage to the Plaza would enable them to bow to their acquaintances and exhibit their last new dresses from New Orleans. Rachela was

---

[22]Panem et Circenses—Bread and circuses
[23]Pan y Toros! [pän′ ê tŏ′rôs]—Bread and bulls!

already prepared for the excursion, and she was not long in attiring Isabel.

"To be sure, the siesta has made you look charming this afternoon," she said, looking steadily into the girl's pretty face, "and this rose silk is enchanting. Santa Maria, how I pity the officers who will have the great fortune to see you this afternoon, and break their hearts for the sight! But you must not look at them, mark! I shall tell the Señora if you do. It is enough if they look at you. And the American way of the Señorita Antonia, which is to bow and smile to every admirer, it will but make more enchanting the becoming modesty of the high-born Mexicaine."

"Keep your tongue still, Rachela. Ah! if you strike me, I will go to my father. He will not permit it. I am not a child to be struck and scolded, and told when to open and shut my eyes."

In the midst of this scene, Antonia entered. She was dressed for the carriage, and the carriage stood at the door waiting, but her face was full of fear.

"Rachela, can you not make some excuse to my mother which will permit us to remain at home? Listen! There is something wrong in the city."

In a moment the three women were on the balcony, intently, anxiously listening. They were aware of a strange confusion in the subtle, amber atmosphere. It was as if they heard the noise of battle afar off. Rachela, without a word, glided away to the Señora. Isabel and Antonia stood hand in hand, listening to the vague trouble and the echo of harsh, grating voices, mingled with the blare of clarions, the roll of drums, and the rattle of scattering

rifle-shots. Yet the noises were so blended together, so
indistinct, so strangely expressive of both laughter and
defiance, that it was impossible to identify or describe
them.

Suddenly a horseman came at a rapid pace towards
the house, and Antonia, leaning over the balcony, saw
him deliver a note to Rachela and then hurry away at the
same reckless speed. The note was from the doctor to
his wife, and it did not tend to allay their anxiety. "Keep
within the house," it said. "There are difficulties in the
city. In an hour or two I will be at home."

But it was near midnight when he arrived, and
Antonia saw that he was a different man. He looked
younger. His blue eyes shone with the light of an invincible determination. His very walk had lost its listless,
gliding tread, and his steps were firm, quick,
and sure.

No one had been able to go to bed until he arrived,
though Isabel slept restlessly in her father's chair, and
the Señora lay upon the couch, drowsing a little between
her frequent attacks of weeping and angry anticipation.
For she was sure it was the Americans. "Anything was
possible with such a man as Sam Houston near the
city."

"Perhaps it is Santa Anna," at length suggested
Antonia. "He has been making trouble ever since I can
remember. He was born with a sword in his hand, I
think."

"Ca! And every American with a rifle in his hand!
Santa Anna is a monster, but at least he fights for his
own country. Texas is not the country of the Americans."

"But, indeed, they believe that Texas is their country—" and to these words Doctor Worth entered.

"What is the matter? What is it, Roberto? I have been made sick with these uncertainties. Why did you not come home at the Angelus?"

"I have had a good reason for my delay, Maria. About three o'clock I received a message from the Señora Alveda, and I visited her. She is in great trouble, and she had not been able to bear it with her usual fortitude. She had fainted."

"Ah, the poor mother! She has a son who will break her heart."

"She made no complaint of Luis. She is distracted about her country, and as I came home I understood why, for she is a very shrewd woman. She perceives that Santa Anna is preparing trouble enough for it."

"Well, then, what is it?"

"When I left her house, I noticed many Americans, as well as many Mexicans, on the streets. They were standing together, too, and there was something in their faces, and in the way their arms were carried, which was very striking and portentous. I fancied they looked coldly on me, and I was troubled by the circumstance. In the Plaza I saw the military band approaching, accompanied by half a dozen officers and a few soldiers. The noise stopped suddenly, and Captain Morello proclaimed as a bando[24] of the highest authoritarian order for all Americans to surrender their arms of every description to the officials and at the places notified."

---

[24]bando—edict

"Very good!"

"Maria, nothing could be worse! Nothing could be more shameful and disastrous. The Americans had evidently been expecting this useless bombast, and ere the words were well uttered, they answered them with a yell of defiance. I do not think more than one proclamation was necessary, but Morello went from point to point in the city and the Americans followed him. I can tell you this, Maria: all the millions in Mexico cannot take their rifles from the 10,000 Americans in Texas able to carry them."

"We shall see! We shall see! But, Roberto, you at least will not interfere in their quarrels. You have never done so hitherto."

"No one has ever proposed to disarm me before, Maria. I tell you frankly, I will not give up a single rifle, or revolver, or weapon of any kind, that I possess. I would rather be slain with them. I have never carried arms before, but I shall carry them now. I apologize to my countrymen for not having them with me this afternoon—Maria! Dear, do not cry in that despairing way."

"You will be killed, Roberto! You will be a rebel! You will be shot like a dog, and then what will become of me and my daughters?"

"You have two sons, Maria. They will avenge their father, and protect their mother and sisters."

"I shall die of shame! I shall die of shame and sorrow!"

"Not of shame, Maria. If I permitted these men to deprive me of my arms, you might well die of shame."

"What is it? Only a gun, or a pistol, that you never use?"

"It is everything! It is honor! It is liberty! It is respect to myself! It is loyalty to my country! It is fidelity to my countrymen! It is true that for many years the garrison has fully protected us, and I have not needed to use the arms in my house. But thousands of husbands and fathers need them hourly to procure food for their children and wives and to protect them from the Indians. One tie binds us. Their cause is my cause. Their country is my country, and their God is my God. Children, am I right or wrong?"

They both stepped swiftly to his side. Isabel laid her cheek against his, and answered him with a kiss. Antonia clasped his hand, stood close to him, and said: "We are all sure that you are right, Father. My mother is weary and sick with anxiety, but she thinks so too. Mother always thinks as you do, Father. Dear mother, here is Rachela with a cup of chocolate, and you will sleep and grow strong before morning."

But the Señora, though she suffered her daughter's caresses, did not answer them, neither did she speak to her husband, though he opened the door for her and stood waiting with a face full of anxious love for a word or a smile from her. And the miserable wife, still more miserable than her husband, noticed that Isabel did not follow her. Never before had Isabel seemed to prefer any society to her mother's, and the unhappy Señora felt the defection, even amid her graver trouble.

But Isabel had seen something new in her father that night—something that touched her awakening soul with admiration. She lingered with him and Antonia, listening with vague comprehension to their conversation, until Rachela called her angrily. An hour afterwards, Antonia stepped cautiously within her room. Isabel slept and smiled, and Antonia whispered a prayer at her side before she went to her own rest.

The waning moon cast a pathetic beauty over the Eden-like land till dawn brought that mystical silence in which every new day is born. Then Robert Worth rose from the chair in which he had been sitting so long, remembering the past and forecasting the future. He walked to the window, opened it, and looked towards the mountains. They had an ethereal hue, a light without rays, a clearness almost polar in its severity. But in some way their appearance infused into his soul calmness and strength.

"Liberty has always been bought with life, and the glory of the greatest nations hanseled[25] with the blood of their founders." This was the thought in his heart, as looking far off to the horizon, he asked hopefully:

> "What then, O God, shall this good land produce
> That Thou art watering it so carefully?"

---

[25]hanseled—launched or begun with ceremony

chapter 5

Juan Returns

*I*t is flesh and blood that makes husbands and wives, fathers and children, and for the next few days these ties were sorely wounded in Robert Worth's house. The Señora was what Rachela called "difficult." In reality, she was angry and sullen. At such times she always went early to mass, said many prayers, and still further irritated herself by unnecessary fasting. But there are few homes which totally escape the visitations of this pious temper in some form or other.

Besides, the Señora, like the ill-tempered prophet, thought she "did well to be angry." She imagined herself deserted and betrayed in all her tenderest feelings, her husband a rebel, her home made desolate, her sons and daughters supporting their father's imprudent views. She could only see one alternative before her; she must choose between her country and her religion, or her husband and children.

True, she had not yet heard from her sons, but she would listen to none of Rachela's hopes regarding them. Thomas had always said yes to all his father's opinions, and how could she expect anything from John when he was being carefully trained in the very principles which everywhere made the Americans so irritating to the Mexican government.

Her husband and Antonia she would not see. Isabel she received in her darkened room, with passionate weeping and many reproaches. The unhappy husband had expected this trouble at the outset. It was one of those domestic thorns which fester and hamper but to which the very best of men have to submit. He could only send pleasant and affectionate messages by Rachela, knowing that Rachela would deliver them with her own modifications of tone and manner.

"The Señor sends his great love to the Señora. If he would do a little as the most wise and tender of spouses wishes him! That would be for the good fortune of every one."

"Ah, Rachela, my heart is broken! Bring me my mantilla. I will go to early mass."

"My Señora, you will take cold; the morning is chill; besides, I have to say the streets will be full of those insolent Americans."

"I shall be glad to take cold, perhaps even to die. And the Americans do not offend women. Even the devil has his good points."

But this morning, early as it was, the streets were empty of Americans. There had been hundreds of them there at the proclamation; there was not one to be seen twelve hours afterwards. At the principal rendezvous of the city, and on the very walls of the Alamo, they had left this characteristic notice:

"To SANTA ANNA:

If you want our arms—take them.

TEN THOUSAND AMERICAN TEXANS."

Robert Worth saw it with an irrepressible emotion of pride and satisfaction. He had faithfully fulfilled his promise to his conscience and, with his rifle across his shoulder and his revolvers and knife in his belt, was taking the road to his office with a somewhat marked deliberation. He was yet a remarkably handsome man— and what man is there that a rifle does not give a kind of nobility to? With an upheld carriage and the light of his soul in his face, he trod the narrow, uneven street like a soldier full of enthusiasm at his own commission.

No one interfered with his solitary parade. He perceived, indeed, a marked approval of it. The Zavalas, Navarros, Garcias, and other prominent citizens ad-dressed him with but a slightly repressed sympathy. They directed his attention with meaning looks to the counter-proclamation of the Americans. They made him understand by the pressure of their hands that they also were on the side of liberty.

As he did not hurry, he met several officers, but they wisely affected not to see what they did not wish to see, for Doctor Worth was a person to whom very wide latitude might be given. To both the military and the civilians his skill was a necessity. The attitude he had taken was privately discussed, but no one publicly acted or even commented upon it. Perhaps he was a little disappointed at this. He had come to a point when a frank avowal of his opinions would be a genuine satisfac-tion.

On the third morning, as he crossed the Plaza, some one called him. The voice made his heart leap; his whole nature responded to it like the strings of a harp to the

sweep of a skilful hand. He turned quickly, and saw two
young men galloping towards him. The foremost figure
was his son—his beloved youngest son—whom he had just
been thinking of as well out of danger, safe and happy in
the peaceful halls of Columbia. And here he was in the
very home of the enemy, and his father was glad of it.

"Why, Jack, my boy!" he cried. "I never thought of you
here." He had his hand on the lad's shoulder and was
gazing into his bright face with happy wonder.

"Father, I had to come. And there are plenty more
coming. Here is my other self—the best fellow that ever
lived: Darius Grant. 'Dare' we call him, Father, for there
is not anything he won't venture if he thinks it worth the
winning. And how is mi madre, and Antonia, and Iza?
Isn't it jolly to see you with a rifle?"

"Well, Dare, Jack, you are both welcome—never so
welcome to Texas as at this hour. Come home at once and
refresh yourselves."

There was so much to tell that at first the conversation
was in fragments and exclamations, and the voices of the
two young men, pitched high and clear in their excitement, went far before them as if impatient of their welcome. Antonia heard them first. She was on the balcony,
standing thoughtful and attentive. It seemed to her as if
in those days she was always listening. Jack's voice was
the loudest, but she heard Dare's first. It vibrated in
midair and fell upon her consciousness, clear and sweet as
a far-away bell.

"That is Dare's voice—HERE."

With swift steps she reached the open door. Rachela
sat in her chair within it.

"The Señorita had better remain within," she said, sullenly, "the sun grows hot."

"Let me pass, Rachela, I am in a hurry."

"To be sure, the Señorita will have her way—good or bad."

Antonia heeded her not; she was hastening down the main avenue toward the gateway. This avenue was hedged on each side with oleanders, and they met in a light, waving arch above her head. At this season they were one mass of pale pink blossoms and dark glossy leaves. The vivid sunshine through them cast a rosy light upon her face and her white gown as she came.

Dare saw her first, and suddenly ceased speaking. He clasped both the pretty hands held out to him and looked at her with eyes full of a loving question, which found its instant answer in her own. Robert Worth needed not the confession which, a few hours later, Grant thought it right to make to him.

When they entered the house together, a happy, noisy group, Rachela had left her chair and was going hurriedly upstairs to tell the Señora her surmise. But Jack passed her with a bound, and was at his mother's side before the heavy old woman had comprehended his passing salutation.

"Madre! Mother, I am here!"

The Señora was on her couch in her darkened room. She had been at the very earliest mass, had a headache, and had come home in a state of rebellion against heaven and earth. But Jack was her idol, the one child for whose presence she continually pined, the one human creature to whose will and happiness she delighted

to sacrifice her own. When she heard his voice she rose
quickly, crying out:

"A miracle! A miracle! Only this morning, my
precious boy, I asked the Holy Mother to pity my sorrows, and send you to me. Oh, Juan! I am too blessed."

Her words were broken into pieces by his kisses. He
knelt at her knees, and stroked her face, and patted her
hands, and did all with such natural fervor and grace
that anything else, or anything less, must have seemed
cold and unfilial.

"Come, madre, and see my friend. I have told him
so much about you, and poor Dare has no mother. I
have promised him that you will be his mother also.
Dare is so good—the finest fellow in all the world; come
down and see Dare, and let us have a real Mexican
dinner, madre. I have not tasted an olla since I left
you."

She could not resist him. She made Rachela lay out
her prettiest dress, and when Jack said "how beautiful
your hair is, mother—no one has hair like you!" she
drew out the great shell pins, and let it fall like a cloud
around her. With a glad pride, she gave Rachela the
order to get out her jewelled comb and gilded fan and
finest mantilla.

Jack's presence drove all the evil spirits out of the
house. The windows were thrown open; the sunshine
came in. One moment he was running after Isabel, the
next he was playing the mandolin. His voice, his laugh,
his quick footstep were everywhere.

In spite of the trouble in the city, there was a real
festival in the house. The Señora came down in her

sweetest temper and her finest garments. She arranged Jack's dinner herself, selected the dishes and gave strict orders about their serving. She took Jack's friend at once into her favor, and Dare thought her wonderfully lovely and gracious. He sat with her on the balcony and talked of Jack, telling her how clever he was, and how all his comrades loved him for his sunny temper and affectionate heart.

It was a happy dinner, lengthened out with merry conversation. Every one thought that a few hours might be given to family love and family joy. It would be good to have the memory of them in the days that were fast coming.

There was not much siesta that day. The Señora, Isabel, and Jack sat together; the Señora dozed a little, but not enough to lose consciousness of Jack's presence and his voice. The father, happy and yet acutely anxious, went to and fro between his children and his study. Antonia and Dare were in the myrtle walk or under the fig tree.

It was understood that the young men were going away in the morning very early; so early that their adieus must be said with their good-nights. It was at this hour that the Señora found courage to ask:

"My Juan, where do you go?"

"To Gonzales, mi madre."

"But why? Oh, Juan, do not desert your madre and your country!

"Desert you, madre! I am your boy to my last breath! My country I love with my whole soul. That is why I have come back to you and to her! She is in trouble, and her sons must stand by her."

"Do not talk with two meanings. Oh, Juan! why do you go to Gonzales?"

"We have heard that Colonel Ugartchea is to be there soon to take away the arms of the Americans. That is not to be endured. If you yourself were a man, you would have been away ere this to help them, I am sure."

"ME!! The Blessed Virgin knows I would cut off my hands and feet first. Juan, listen to me, dear one! You are a Mexican."

"My heart is Mexican, for it is yours. But I must stand with my father and my brother, and with my American compatriots. Are we slaves, that we must give up our arms? No, but if we gave them up we should deserve to be slaves."

"What a trouble about a few guns! One would think the Mexicans wanted the wives and children of the Americans. Juan, my darling, you are my last hope. Your brother was born with an American heart. He has even become a heretic. Fray Ignatius says he went into the Colorado and was what they call immersed; he that was baptized with holy water by the thrice holy bishop of Durango. My beloved one, go and see Fray Ignatius; late as it is, he will rise and counsel you.

"My heart, my conscience, my country, my father, my brother, Santa Anna's despotism—these have already counselled me."

"Speak no more. I see that you also are a rebel and a heretic. Mother of sorrows, give me thy compassion!" Then, turning to Juan, she cried out: "May God pardon me for having brought into this world such ingrates! Go from me! You have broken my heart!"

He fell at her feet and, in spite of her reluctance, took her hands—

"Sweetest mother, wait but a little while. You will see that we are right. Do not be cross with Juan. I am going away. Kiss me, madre. Kiss me, and give me your blessing."

"No, I will not bless you. I will not kiss you. You want what is impossible—what is wicked."

"I want freedom."

"And to get freedom you tread upon your mother's heart. Let loose my hands. I am weary to death of this everlasting talk of freedom. I think indeed that the Americans know but two words: freedom and dollars. Ring for Rachela. She, at least, is faithful to me."

"Not till you kiss me, Mother. Do not send me away unblessed and unloved. That is to doom me to misfortune. Mi madre, I beg this favor from you." He had risen, but he still held her hands, and he was weeping as innocent young men are not ashamed to weep.

If she had looked at him! Oh, if she had but once looked at his face, she could not have resisted its beauty, its sorrow, its imploration! But she would not look. She drew her hands angrily away from him. She turned her back upon her suppliant son and imperiously summoned Rachela.

"Good-by, mi madre."

"Good-by, mi madre!"

She would not turn to him, or answer him a word.

"Mi madre, here comes Rachela! Say 'God bless you, Juan.' It is my last word, sweet mother!"

She neither moved nor spoke. The next moment Rachela entered, and the wretched woman abandoned herself to her care with vehement sobs and complainings.

Jack was inexpressibly sorrowful. He went into the garden, hoping in its silence and solitude to find some relief. He loved his mother with his strongest affection. Every one of her sobs wrung his heart. Was it right to wound and disobey her for the sake of freedom? Mother was a certain good; freedom only a glorious promise. Mother was a living fact; freedom an intangible idea.

But men have always fought more passionately for ideas than for facts! Tyrants are safe while they touch only silver and gold, but when they try to bind a man's ideals—the freedom of his citizenship—the purity of his faith—he will die to preserve them in their integrity.

Besides, freedom for every generation has but her hour. If that hour is not seized, no other may come for the men who have suffered it to pass. But mother would grow more loving as the days went by. This was ever the end of Jack's reasoning; for no man knows how deep the roots of his nature strike into his native land, until he sees her in the grasp of a tyrant, and hears her crying to him for deliverance.

The struggle left the impress on his face. He passed a boundary in it. Certain boyish feelings and graces would never again be possible to him. He went into the house, weary and longing for companionship that would comfort or strengthen him. Only Isabel was in the parlor. She appeared to be asleep among the sofa cushions, but she opened her eyes wide as he took a chair beside her.

"I have been waiting to see you again, Juan; do you think this trouble will last very long?"

"It will be over directly, Iza. Do not fret yourself about it, angel mio. The Americans are great fighters, and their quarrel is just. Well, then, it will be settled by the good God quickly."

"Rachela says that Santa Anna has sent a million men to fight the Americans. Some they will cut in pieces, and some are to be sent to the mines to work in chains."

"God is not dead of old age, Iza. Santa Anna is a miraculous tyrant. He has committed every crime under heaven, but I think he will not cut the Americans in pieces."

"And if the Americans should even make him go back to Mexico!"

"I think that is very possible."

"What then, Juan?"

"He would pay for some of his crimes here—the rest he would settle in purgatory.[26] And you, too, Iza, are you with the Americans?"

"Luis Alveda says they are right."

"Oh-h! I see! So Luis is to be my brother, too. Is that so, little dear?"

"Have you room in your heart for him? Or has this Dare Grant filled it?"

---

[26]purgatory—in Roman Catholic tradition, a place of temporary punishment for the souls of repentant sinners before they can enter heaven

"If I had twenty sisters, I should have room for twenty brothers, if they were like Dare and Luis. But, indeed, Luis had his place there before I knew Dare."

"Perhaps you may see him soon; he is with Señor Sam Houston. Señor Houston was here not a week ago. Will you think of that? And the mother and uncle of Luis are angry at him; he will be disinherited, and we shall be very poor, I think. But there is always my father, who loves Luis."

"Luis will win his own inheritance. I think you will be very rich."

"And, Juan, if you see Luis, say to him, 'Iza thinks of you continually.'"

At this moment Rachela angrily called her charge—

"Are you totally and forever wicked, disobedient one? Two hours I have been kept waiting. Very well! The Sisters are the only duenna for you—back to the convent you shall go to-morrow. The Señora is of my mind, also."

"My father will not permit it. I will go to my father. And think of this, Rachela: I am no longer to be treated like a baby." But she kissed Juan 'farewell,' and went away without further dispute.

The handsome room looked strangely lonely and desolate when the door had closed behind her. Jack rose and roughly shook himself, as if by that means he hoped to throw off the oppression and melancholy that was invading even his light heart. Hundreds of moths were dashing themselves to death against the high glass shade that covered the blowing candles from them. He stood and looked at their hopeless efforts to reach the flame.

He had an unpleasant thought; one of those thoughts which have the force of a presentiment. He put it away with annoyance, muttering, "It is time enough to meet misfortune when it comes."

The sound of a footstep made him stand erect and face the door.

It was only a sleepy servant with a request that he would go to his father's study. A different mental atmosphere met him there. The doctor was walking up and down the room, and Dare and Antonia sat together at the open window.

"Your father wants to hear about our journey, Jack. Take my chair and tell him what happened. Antonia and I will walk within hearing; a roof makes me restless such a night as this." The waning moon had risen, and a cool wind from the Gulf was shaking a thousand scents from the trees and the flowering shrubs.

The change was made with the words, and the doctor sat down beside his son. "I was asking, Jack, how you knew so much about Texan affairs, and how you came so suddenly to take part in them?"

"Indeed, father, we could not escape knowing. The Texan fever was more or less in every young man's blood. One night Dare had a supper at his rooms, and there were thirty of us present. A man called Faulkner—a fine fellow from Nacogdoches—spoke to us. How do you think he spoke, when his only brother, a lad of twenty, is working in a Mexican mine loaded with chains?"

"For what?"

"He said one day that 'the natural boundaries of the United States are the Atlantic and Pacific oceans.' He

was sent to the mines for the words. Faulkner's only
hope for him is in the independence of Texas. He had us
on fire in five minutes—all but Sandy McDonald, who
loves to argue, and therefore took the Mexican side."

"What could he say for it?"

"He said it was a very unjustlike thing to make
Mexico give her American settlers in Texas two hundred
and twenty-four millions of acres just because they
thought a change of government best for their own
interests."

"The Americans settled in Texas under the solemn
guarantee of the constitution of 1824. How many of
them would have built homes under a tyrannical despotism like that Santa Anna is now forcing upon them?"
asked the doctor, warmly.

"McDonald said, 'There is a deal of talk about freedom among you Americans, and it just means nothing at
all.' You should have seen Faulkner! He turned on him
like a tornado. 'How should you know anything about
freedom, McDonald?' he cried. 'You are in feudal darkness in the Highlands of Scotland. You have only just
emigrated into freedom. But we Americans are born
free! If you cannot feel the difference between a federal
constitution and a military and religious despotism, there
is simply no use talking to you. How would you like to
find yourself in a country where suddenly trial by jury
and the exercise of your religion was denied you? Of
course you could abandon the home you had built, and
the acres you had bought and put under cultivation, and
thus make some Mexican heir to your ten years' labor.
Perhaps a Scot, for conscience' sake, would do this.' "

"And what answer made he?"

"He said, 'A Scot kens how to grip tight to ten years' labor as well as yoursel, Faulkner, and neither man nor de'il can come between him and his religion. But—' 'BUT,' shouted Faulkner; 'there is no BUT! It is God and our right! God and our right, against priestcraft and despotism!' "

"Then every one of us leaped to our feet, and we swore to follow Faulkner to Texas at an hour's notice. Sandy said we were 'a parcel of fools,' but then, would you believe it, Father, when our boat was leaving the pier, amid the cheers and hurrahs of thousands, Sandy leaped on the boat and joined us?"

"What did he say then?"

"He said, 'I am a born fool to go with you, but I think there is a kind o' witchcraft in that word TEXAS. It has been stirring me up morning and night like the voice o' the charmer, and I be to follow it though I ken well enough it isna' leading me in the paths o' peace and pleasantness!' "

"Did you find the same enthusiasm outside of New York?"

"All along the Ohio and Mississippi we gathered recruits; and at Randolph, sixty miles above Memphis, we were joined by David Crockett."

"Jack!"

"True, father! And then at every landing we took on men. For at every landing Crockett spoke to the people and, as we stopped very often, we were cheered all the way down the river. The *Mediterranean*, though the biggest boat on it, was soon crowded. But at Helena,

Crockett and a great number of the leading men of the
expedition got off. Since Dare and Crockett had become friends, I followed them."

"Where did you go?"

"We went ostensibly to a big barbecue at John
Bowie's plantation, which is a few miles below Helena.
Invitations to this barbecue had been sent hundreds of
miles throughout the surrounding country. We met
parties from the depths of the Arkansas wilderness and
the furthest boundaries of the Choctaw nation coming
to it. There were raftsmen from the Mississippi, from
the White, and the St. Francis rivers. There were
planters from Louisiana and Tennessee. There were
woodsmen from Kentucky. There were envoys from
New Orleans, Washington, and all the great Eastern
cities."

"I had an invitation myself, Jack."

"I wish you had accepted it. It was worth the journey.
There never was and there never will be such a barbecue
again. Thousands were present. The woods were full of
sheds and temporary buildings, and platforms for the
speakers."

"Who were the speakers?"

"Crockett, Hawkins, General Montgomery, Colonel
Beauford, the three brothers Cheatham, Doc. Bennet,
and many others. When the woods were illuminated at
night with pine knots, you may imagine the scene and
the wild enthusiasm that followed their eloquence. I
suppose you know, Father," said Jack, sinking his voice
to a whisper, "that we have still more powerful backers."

"General Gaines?"

"Well, he has a large body of United States troops at Nacogdoches. He says they are to protect the people of Navasola from the Indians."

"But Navasola is twenty-nine miles west of Nacog-doches."

"Navasola is in Texas. Very well! If the United States feel it to be their duty to protect the people of Navasola, it seems they already consider Texas within their boundary."

"You think the Indians a mere pretext?"

"Of course. Crockett has with him an autograph letter from President Jackson, introducing him as 'a God-chosen patriot.' President Jackson already sees Texas in the Union, and Gaines understands that if the American-Texans should be repulsed by Santa Anna, and fall back upon him, that he may then gather them under his standard and lead them forward to victory—and the conquest of Texas. Father, you will see the Stars and Stripes on the palaces of Mexico yet."

"Do not talk too fast, Jack. Now, go lie down on my bed. In four hours you must leave, if you want to reach Gonzales tonight!"

chapter 6

Robert Worth Is Disarmed

The keenest sufferings entailed by war are not on the battlefield, nor in the hospital. They are in the household. There are the maimed affections, the slain hopes, the broken ties of love. Before a shot had been fired in the war of Texan independence, the battle had begun in Robert Worth's household.

The young men lay down to rest, but he sat watching the night away. There was a melancholy sleepiness in it; the mockingbirds had ceased singing; the chirping insects had become weary. Only the clock, with its regular "tick, tick," kept the watch with him.

When it was near dawn, he lifted a candle and went into the room where Jack and Dare were sleeping. Dare did not move; Jack opened his eyes wide and smiled brightly at the intruder.

"Well, Father?"

"It is time to get up, Jack. Tell Dare."

In a few minutes both came to him. They ate standing, speaking very little and almost in whispers; and then the doctor went with them to the stable. He helped Jack to saddle his horse. He found a sad pleasure in coming so close to him. Once their cheeks touched, and the touch brought the tears to his eyes.

With his hand on the saddle, Jack paused and said, softly, "Father, tell mi madre my last look at the house, my last thought in leaving it, was for her. She would not kiss me or bless me last night. Ask her to kiss you for me," and then the lad broke fairly down. The moment had come in which love could find no utterance, and must act. He flung his arm around his father's neck and kissed him. The father wept also, and yet spoke brave words to both as he walked with them to the gate and watched them ride into the thick mist lying upon the prairie like a cloud.

He thought no one had seen the boys leave but himself, but through the lattices two sorrowful women also watched their departure. The Señora, as wakeful as her husband, had heard the slight movements, the unusual noises of that early hour, and had divined the cause of them. She looked at Rachela. The woman had fallen into the dead sleep of exhaustion, and she would not have to parry her objections and warnings. Unshod, and in her night-dress, she slipped through the corridor to the back of the house, and tightly clasping her rosary in her hands, she stood behind the lattice and watched her boy away.

He turned in his saddle just before he passed the gate, and she saw his young face lifted with an unconscious, anxious love, to the very lattice at which she stood: in the dim light it had a strange pallor. The misty air blurred and made all indistinct. It was like seeing her Jack in some woeful dream. If he had been dead, such a vision of him might have come to her from the shadow land.

Usually her grief was noisy and imperative of sympathy. But this morning she could not cry nor lament. She went softly back to her room and sat down, with her crucifix before her aching eyes. Yet she could not say her usual prayers. She could not remember anything but Jack's entreaty—"Kiss me, mi madre! Bless me, mi madre!" She could not see anything but that last rapid turn in the saddle, and that piteous young face, showing so weird and dreamlike through the gray mist of the early dawn.

Antonia had watched with her. Dare, also, had turned, but there had been something about Dare's attitude far more cheery and hopeful. On the previous night Antonia had put some sprays of rosemary in his hat band "to bring good, and keep away evil on a journey"; and as he turned and lifted his hat he put his lips to them. He had the belief that from some point his Antonia was watching him. He conveyed to her, by the strength of his love and his will, the assurance of all their hopes.

That day Doctor Worth did not go out. The little bravado of carrying arms was impossible to him. It was not that his courage had failed, or that he had lost a tittle of his convictions, but he was depressed by the uncertainty of his position and duty, and he was, besides, in the thrall of that intangible anxiety which we call *presentiment*.[27]

Yet, however dreary life is, it must go on. The brave-hearted cannot drop daily duty. On the second day the

---

[27]presentiment—a feeling that something is about to happen

doctor went to his office again, and Antonia arranged the meals and received company, and did her best to bring the household into peaceful accord with the new elements encroaching on it from all sides.

But the Señora was more "difficult" than even Rachela had ever seen her before. She did not go to church, but Fray Ignatius spent a great deal of time with her, and his influence was not any more conciliating than that of early masses and much fasting.

He said to her, indeed: "My daughter, you have behaved with the fortitude of a saint. It would have been more than a venial sin, if you had kissed and blessed a rebel in the very act of his rebellion. The Holy Mary will reward and comfort you."

But the Señora was not sensible of the reward and comfort, and she did feel most acutely the cruel wound she had given her mother love. Neither prayers nor penance availed her. She wanted to see Jack. She wanted to kiss him a hundred times and to bless him with every kiss—and it did not help her to be told that these longings were the suggestions of the Evil One, and not to be listened to.

The black-robed monk, gliding about the house with downcast eyes and folded hands, had never seemed to Robert Worth so objectionable. He knew that he kept the breach open between himself and his wife—that he thought it a point of religious duty to do so. He knew that he was gradually isolating the wretched woman from her husband and children, and that the continual repetition of prayers and penances did not give her any adequate comfort for the wrong she was doing her affections.

The city was also in a condition of the greatest excitement. The soldiers in the Alamo were under arms. Their officers had evidently received important advices from Mexico. General Cos, the brother-in-law of Santa Anna, was now in command, and it was said immense reinforcements were hourly looked for. The drifting American population had entirely vanished, but its palpable absence inspired the most thoughtful of the people with fear instead of security.

Nor were the military by any means sure of the loyalty of the city. It was well known that a large proportion of the best citizens hated the despotism of Santa Anna, and that if the Americans attacked San Antonio, they would receive active sympathy. Party feeling was no longer controllable. Men suspected each other. Duels were a constant occurrence and families were torn to pieces, for the monks supported Santa Anna with all their influence, and there were few women who dared to disobey them.

Into the midst of this turbulent, touchy community, there fell one morning a word or two which set it on fire. Doctor Worth was talking on the Plaza with Señor Lopez Navarro. A Mexican soldier, with his yellow cloak streaming out behind him, galloped madly towards the Alamo and left the news there. It spread like wildfire. "There had been a fight at Gonzales, and the Americans had kept their arms. They had also put the Mexicans to flight."

"And more," added a young Mexican coming up to the group which had gathered about Worth and Navarro, "Stephen Austin has escaped. He arrived at Gonzales at the very moment of victory. Moreover, Americans are pouring into Gonzales from every quarter."

An officer tapped Doctor Worth on the shoulder. "Señor Doctor, your arms. General Cos hopes, in the present extremity, you will set an example of obedience."

"I will not give up my arms. In the present extremity my arms are the greatest need I have."

"Then Señor—it is a great affliction to me—I must arrest you."

He was led away amid the audible murmurs of the men who filled the streets. There needed but someone to have said the word, and they would have taken him forcibly from the military. A great crowd followed him to the gates of the Alamo, for there was scarcely a family in San Antonio of which this good doctor was not an adopted member. The arrest of their favorite confessor would hardly have enraged them more.

Fray Ignatius brought the news to the Señora. Even he was affected by it. Never before had Antonia seen him walk except with thoughtful and deliberate steps. She wondered at his appearance—at its suppressed hurry. Something in it struck her as suppressed satisfaction.

Antonia met him at the door. He said an *Ave Maria* as he crossed the threshold and gave her his hand to kiss. She looked wonderingly in his face, for unless it was a special visit, he never called so near the Angelus. Still, it is difficult to throw off a habit of obedience formed in early youth; and she did not feel as if she could break through the chill atmosphere of the man and ask: "For what reason have you come, father?"

A long, shrill shriek from the Señora was the first
answer to the fearful question in her heart. In a few
moments she was at her mother's door. Rachela knelt
outside it, telling her rosary. She stolidly kept her place,
and a certain instinct for a moment prevented Antonia
from interrupting her. But the passionate words of her
mother, blending with the low, measured tones of the
priest, were something far more positive.

"Let me pass you, Rachela. What is the matter with
my mother?"

The woman was absorbed in her supplications, and
Antonia opened the door. Isabel followed her. They
found themselves in the presence of an angry sorrow that
appalled them. The Señora had torn her lace mantilla
into shreds, and they were scattered over the room as she
had flung them from her hands in her frantic walk about
it. The large shell comb that confined her hair was
trodden to pieces, and her long coils had fallen about her
face and shoulders. Her bracelets, her chain of gold, her
brooch and rings were scattered on the floor, and she
was standing in the center of it, like an enraged creature,
tearing her handkerchief into strips as an emphasis to
her passionate denunciations.

"It serves him right! It serves him right! He must
carry arms! HE, TOO! when it was forbidden! I am glad
he is arrested! Oh, Roberto! Roberto!"

"Patience, my daughter! This is the hand of God.
What can you do but submit?"

"What is it, mi madre?" and Isabel put her arms
around her mother with the words *mi madre*. "Tell Isabel
your sorrow."

"Your father is arrested—taken to the Alamo—he will
be sent to the mines. I told him so! I told him so! He
would not listen to me! How wicked he has been!"

"What has my father done, Fray Ignatius? Why have
they arrested him?"

The priest turned to Antonia with a cold face. He did
not like her. He felt that she did not believe in him.

"Señorita, he has committed a treason. A good
citizen obeys the law; Señor Worth has defied it."

"Pardon, father, I cannot believe it."

"A great forbearance has been shown him, but the
end of mercy comes. As he persisted in wearing arms, he
has been taken to the Alamo and disarmed."

"It is a great shame! An infamous shame and
wrong!" cried Antonia. "What right has anyone to take
my father's arms? No more than they have to take his
purse or his coat."

"General Santa Anna—"

"General Santa Anna is a tyrant and a thief. I care
not who says different."

"Antonia! Shameless one!"

"Mother, do not strike me." Then she took her
mother's hands in her own, and led her to a couch,
caressing her as she spoke—

"Don't believe anyone—ANYONE, mother, who says
wrong of my father. You know that he is the best of men.
Rachela! Come here instantly. The rosary is not the
thing, now. You ought to be attending to the Señora.
Get her some valerian and some coffee, and come and
remove her clothing. Fray Ignatius, we will beg you to
leave us to-night to ourselves."

"Your mother's sin, in marrying a heretic, has now found her out. It is my duty to make her see her fault."

"My mother had a dispensation from one greater than you."

"Oh, father, pray for me! I accuse myself! I accuse myself! Oh, wretched woman! Oh, cruel husband!"

"Mother, you have been a very happy woman. You have had the best husband in the world. Do not reproach my father for the sins of others. Do not desert him when he is in the power of a human tiger. Let us think of something to be done for his help! I will see the Navarros, the Garcias, Judge Valdez; I will go to the Plaza and call on the thousands he has cured and helped to set him free."

"You will make of yourself something not to be spoken of. This is the judgment of God, my daughter."

"It is the judgment of a wicked man, Fray Ignatius. My mother is not now able to listen to you. Isabel, come here and comfort her." Isabel put her cheek to her mother's; kissed her face; and, with childlike sweetness, murmured words of consolation and hope.

Fray Ignatius watched her with a cold scrutiny. He was saying to himself, "It is the fruit of sin. I warned the Señora, when she married this heretic, that trouble would come of it. Very well, it has come." Then like a flash a new thought invaded his mind—If the Señor Doctor disappeared forever, why not induce the Señora and her daughters to go into a religious house? There was a great deal of money. The Church could use it well.

Antonia did not understand the thought, but she understood its animus,[28] and again she requested his withdrawal. This time she went close to him and bravely looked straight into his eyes. Their scornful gleam sent a chill to her heart like that of cold steel. At that moment she understood that she had turned a passive enemy into an active one.

He went, however, without further parley, stopping only to warn the Señora against the sin "of standing with the enemies of God and the Holy Church," and to order Isabel to recite for her mother's pardon and comfort a certain number of aves and paternosters. Antonia went with him to the door, and ere he left he blessed her, and said: "The Señorita will examine her soul and see her sin. Then the ever merciful Church will hear her confession, and give her the satisfying penance."

Antonia bowed in response. When people are in great domestic sorrow, self-examination is a superfluous advice. She listened a moment to his departing footsteps, shivering as she stood in the darkness, for a norther[29] had sprung up, and the cold was severe. She only glanced into the pleasant parlor where the table was laid for dinner, and a great fire of cedar logs was throwing red, dancing lights over the white linen and the shining silver and glass. The chairs were placed around the table; her father's at the head. It had a forsaken air that was unendurable.

---

[28]animus—disposition or ill will
[29]norther—a sudden, cold wind from the north

The dinner hour was now long past. It would be folly to attempt the meal. How could she and Isabel sit down alone and eat, while their father was in prison and their mother was frantic with a loss which she was warned it was sinful to mourn over. Antonia had a soul made for extremities and not afraid to face them, but invisible hands controlled her. What could a woman do, whom society had forbidden to do anything but endure the pangs of patience?

The Señora could offer no suggestions. She was not indeed in a mood to think of her resources. A spiritual dread was upon her. And with this mingled an intense sense of personal wrong from her husband. 'Had she not begged him to be passive? And he had put an old rifle before her and her daughters! It was all that Señor Houston's doing. She had an assurance of that.' She invoked a thousand maledictions on him. She recalled, with passionate reproaches, Jack's infidelity to her and his God and his country. Her anger passed from one subject to another constantly, finding in all, even in the lukewarmness of Antonia and Isabel, and in their affection for men who were also rebels, an accumulating reason for a stupendous reproach against herself, her husband, her children, and her unhappy fate. Her whole nature was in revolt.

Isabel wept so violently that she angered still further the tearless suffering of her mother. "What are you weeping for?" she cried. "Will tears do any good? Do I weep? God has forbidden me to weep for the wicked. Yet how I suffer! Mary, mother of sorrows, pity me!"

She sent Isabel away. Her sobs were not to be borne. And very soon she felt Antonia's white face and silent companionship to be just as unendurable. She would be alone. Not even Rachela would she have near her. She put out all the lights but the taper above a large crucifix, and at its foot she sat down in tearless abandon, alone with her reproaches and her remorse.

Antonia watched with her mother, though shut out from her presence. She feared for a state of mind so barren of affection, so unsoftened by tears. Besides, it was the climax of a condition which had continued ever since she had sent her boy away without a word of love. In the dim corridor outside she sat still, listening for any noise or movement which might demand help or sympathy. It was not nine o'clock, but the time lengthened itself out beyond endurance. Even yet she had hope of some word from her father. Surely, they would let him send some word to them!

She heard the murmur of voices downstairs, and she thought angrily of Rachela, and Molly, and Manuel, "making a little confidence together" over their trouble, and spicing their evening gossip with the strange thing that had happened to the Señor Doctor. She knew that Rachela and Manuel would call him heretic and Americano, and, by authority of these two words, accuse him of every crime.

Thinking with a swelling heart of these things, she heard the door open, and a step slowly and heavily ascend the stairs. Before she had time to wonder at it, her father came in sight. There was a shocking change in his air and appearance, but as he was evidently going to her mother's room, she shrank back and sat motionless so as not to attract his attention.

Then she went to the parlor, and had the fire renewed and food put upon the table. She was sure that he would need it, and she believed he would be glad to talk over with her the events of the afternoon.

The Señora was still sitting at the foot of the crucifix when her husband opened the door. She had not been able to pray; ave and paternoster alike had failed her. Her rebellious grief filled every corner of her heart. She understood that someone had entered the room, and she thought of Rachela. But she found a kind of comfort in the dull stupor of grief she was indulging, and she would not break its spell by lifting her head.

"Maria."

She rose up quickly and stood gazing at him.

She did not shriek or exclaim; her surprise controlled her. And also her terror; for his face was white as death, and it wore an expression of angry despair that terrified her.

"Roberto! How you have tortured me! I have nearly died! Fray Ignatius said you had been sent to prison."

She spoke as calmly as a frightened child; sad and hesitating. If he had taken her in his arms she would have sobbed her grief away there.

But Robert Worth was at that hour possessed by another passion, tyrannical and insatiable—and it would take notice of nothing that did not minister to it.

"Maria, they have taken my arms from me. Miserable cowards! I refused to give them up! They held my hands and robbed me—robbed me of my manhood and honor! I begged them to shoot me ere they did it, and they spoke courteously and regretted this, and hoped that, till I felt that it would be a joy to strangle them."

"Roberto! You have me!"

"I want my rifle and all it represents. I want myself back again. Maria, until then, I am not worthy to be any good woman's husband!"

"Roberto, dearest! It is not your fault."

"It is my fault. I have waited too long. My sons showed me my duty—my soul urged me to do it. I deserve the shame. I should have gone to Gonzalez with Jack."

The Señora stood speechless, wringing her hands. Her own passion was puny beside the sternness, the reality, and the intensity of the quiet rage before her. She was completely mastered by it. She forgot all but the evident agony she could neither mistake nor console.

"I have come to say 'farewell,' Maria. We have been very happy together—"

"Oh, Roberto, my husband! Leave me not!"

"I am going for my arms. I will take them a hundred-fold from those who have robbed me. I swear I will!"

"You do not love me. What are these Americans to you? I am your wife. Your Maria—"

"These Americans are my brothers—my sons. My mother is an American woman."

"And I?"

"You are my wife—my dear wife! And I love you—God Almighty knows how well I love you. But we must part now, at least for a short time. I must go."

"Go? But where?"

"I am going to join General Houston."

"I thought so. I knew it. The accursed one! Oh, that I had him here again! I would bury my stiletto in his heart! Stay till daylight, Roberto. I have so much to say, dearest."

"I cannot. I have stayed too long. And now I must ride without a gun or knife to protect me. Any Indian that I meet can scalp me. Do you understand now what disarming means, Maria? If I had gone with my boy, with my brave Jack, I could at least have sold my life to its last drop."

"In the morning, Roberto, Lopez Navarro will get you a gun. Oh, if you must go, do not go unarmed! There are ten thousand Comanche between here and the Brazos."

"How could I look Lopez Navarro in the face? Or any other man? No—I must win back my arms before I can walk the streets of San Antonio again."

She clung to his neck, to his hands, to his feet; she made his farewell an unspeakable agony. At last he laid her upon her couch, sobbing and shrieking like a child in an extremity of physical anguish. But he did not blame her. Her impetuosities, her unreasonable extravagances, were a part of her nature, her race, and her character. He did not expect a weak, excitable woman to become suddenly a creature of flame and steel.

But it was a wonderful rest to his exhausted body and soul to turn from her to Antonia. She led him quietly to his chair by the parlor fire. She gave him food and drink. She listened patiently, but with a living sympathy, to his wrong. She endorsed, with a clasp of his hand and a smile, his purpose, and she said, almost cheerfully:

"You have not given up all your arms, Father. When I first heard of the edict, I hid in my own room the rifle, the powder, and the shot, which were in your study. Paola has knives in the stable; plenty of them. You can get one from him."

Good news is a very relative thing. This information made the doctor feel as if all were now easy and possible. The words he said to her, Antonia never forgot. They sang in her heart like music, and led her on through many a difficult path. The conversation then turned upon money matters, and Antonia received the key to his study and full directions as to the gold and papers secreted there.

Then Isabel was awakened, and the rifle brought down. Paola saddled the fleetest horse in the stable, and after one solemn five minutes with his daughters, Robert Worth rode away into the midnight darkness, and into a chaos of public events of which no man living could forecast the outcome.

Rode away from wife and children and home, leaving behind him the love and labor of his lifetime. For what? For justice, for freedom of thought and action, for the rights of his manhood, for the brotherhood of race and religion and country. Antonia and Isabel stood hand in hand at the same lattice from which the Señora had watched her son away, and in a dim, uncertain manner these thoughts connected themselves in each mind with the same mournful inquiry: Is it worthwhile?

As the beat of the horse's hoofs died away, they turned. The night was cold but clear, and the sky appeared so high that their eyes throbbed as they gazed upward at the grand arch, sprinkled with suns and worlds. Suddenly into the tranquil spaces there was flung a sound of joy and revelry, and the girls stepped to a lattice at the end of the corridor and looked out.

The residencia of Don Salvo Valasco was clearly visible from this site. They saw that it was illuminated throughout. Lovely women, shining with jewels, and soldiers in scarlet and gold, were chatting through the graceful movements of the danza. The misty beauty of white lace mantillas, the glitter and color of fans and festival dresses, made a moving picture of great beauty.

As they watched it there was a cessation of the dance, followed by the rapid sweep of a hand across the strings of a guitar. Then a group of officers stepped together, and a great wave of melodious song, solemn and triumphant, thrilled the night. It was the national hymn. Antonia and Isabel knew it. Every word beat upon their hearts. The power of association, the charm of a stately, fervent melody was upon them.

"It is Señor Higadillos who leads," whispered Isabel, as a resonant voice, powerful and sweet, cried—

>   "O list to the summons! The blood of our sires,
>   Boils high in our veins, and to vengeance in-
>   spires!
>   Who bows to the yoke? who bends to the blow?"

and, without a moment's hesitation, the answer came in a chorus of enthusiastic cadences—

>   "No hero will bend, no Mexican bow;

Our country in tears sends her sons to the fight,
To conquer, or die, for our land and our right."
"You see, the Mexicans think THEY are in the right—
THEY are patriots also, Antonia."

The sorrowful girl spoke like a puzzled child, fretfully
and uncertainly, and Antonia led her silently away. What
could she answer? And when she remembered the dear
fugitive, riding alone through the midnight—riding now
for life and liberty—she could not help the uprising again
of that cold benumbing question—Is it worthwhile?

chapter **7**

A Meeting at Midnight

*T*he gathering at Don Valasco's was constantly
repeated in various degrees of splendor among
the loyal Mexicans of the city. They were as fully convinced of the justice of their cause as the Americans
were. "They had graciously permitted Americans to
make homes in their country; now they wanted not only
to build heretic churches and sell heretic Bibles, but also
to govern Texas after their own fashion." From a Mexican point of view the American settlers were a godless,
atheistical, quarrelsome set of ingrates. For eaten bread
is soon forgotten, and Mexicans disliked to remember

that their own independence had been won by the aid
of the very men they were now trying to force into
subjection.

The two parties were already in array in every
house in the city. The Señora at variance with her
daughters, their Irish cook quarrelling with their
Mexican servants, only represented a state of things
nearly universal. And after the failure of the Mexicans
at Gonzales to disarm the Americans, the animosity
constantly increased.

In every church, the priests—more bitter, fierce, and
revengeful than either the civil or military powers—
urged on the people an exterminating war. A black flag
waved from the Missions, and fired every heart with an
unrelenting vengeance and hatred. To slay a heretic
was a free pass through the dolorous pains of purgatory. For the priesthood foresaw that the triumph of
the American element meant the triumph of freedom of
conscience and the abolition of their own despotism.
To them the struggle was one involving all the privileges
of their order, and so they urged on the fight with
passionate denunciations of the foe and with magnificent promises of spiritual favors and blessings. In the
fortress, the plaza, the houses, the churches, the streets,
their fiery words kept society in a ferment.

But through all this turmoil the small duties of life
went on. Soldiers were parading the streets and keeping watch on the flat roofs of the houses; men were
solemnly swearing allegiance to Santa Anna, or flying
by night to the camp of the Americans; life and death
were held at a pin's fee. But eating, dressing, dancing,

and flirting were pursued with an eagerness typical of
pleasure caught in the passing.

And every hour these elements gathered intensity.
The always restless populace of San Antonio was at a
feverish point of impatience. They wanted the war at
their own doors. They wanted the quarrel fought out on
their own streets. Business took a secondary place. Men
fingered weapons and dreamed of blood, until the temper of the town was as boisterous and vehement as the
temper of the amphitheatre when impatiently waiting for
the bulls and the matadores.

Nor was it possible for Antonia to lock the door upon
this pervading spirit. After Doctor Worth's flight, it
became necessary for her to assume control over the
household. She had promised him to do so, and she was
resolved, in spite of all opposition, to follow out his
instructions. But it was by no means an easy task.

Fray Ignatius had both the Señora and Rachela
completely under his subjection. Molly, the Irish cook,
was already dissatisfied. The doctor had saved her life
and given her a good home and generous wages, and
while the doctor was happy and prosperous Molly was
accordingly grateful. But a few words from the priest set
affairs in a far different light to her. She was a true
Catholic; the saints sent the heretic doctor to help. It
was therefore the saints to whom gratitude was due.
Had she not earned her good wage? And would not Don
Angel Sandoval give her a still larger sum? Or even the
Brothers at the Mission of San Jose? Molly listened to
these words with a complacent pleasure. She reflected
that it would be much more agreeable to her to be where

she could entirely forget that she had ever been
hungry and friendless, and lying at death's door.

Antonia knew also that Rachela was at heart
unfaithful, and soon the conviction was forced on her
that servants are never faithful beyond the line of
their own interest—that it is, indeed, against certain
primary laws of nature to expect it. Certainly, it was
impossible to doubt that there was in all their depend-
ents a kind of satisfaction in their misfortunes.

The doctor had done them favors—how unpleasant was their memory! The Señora had offended
them by the splendor of her dress, and her complacent air of happiness. Antonia's American ways and
her habit of sitting for hours with a book in her hand
were a great irritation.

"She wishes to be thought wiser than other
women—as wise as even a holy priest—SHE! who
never goes to mass and is nearly a heretic," said the
house steward. "As for the Señorita Isabel, a little
trouble will be good for her! The way she has been
pampered and petted! It is an absurdity. 'Little dear,'
and 'angel,' are the hardest words she hears. Si! if
God did not mercifully abate a little the rich they
would grow to be 'almightys.' "

This was the tone of the conversation among the
household servants. It was not an unnatural tone, but
it was a very unhappy one. People cannot escape
from the mood of mind they habitually indulge, or
from the animus of the words they habitually use, and
Antonia felt and understood the antagonistic atmosphere.

The Señora, in a plain black serge gown and black rebozo[30] over her head, spent her time in prayers and penances. The care of her household had always been delegated to her steward and to Rachela, while the duties that more especially belonged to her had been fulfilled by her husband and by Antonia. In many respects she was but a grown-up baby. And so, in this great extremity, the only duty which pressed upon her was the idea of supplicating the saints to take charge of her unhappy affairs.

And Fray Ignatius was daily more hard with her. Antonia suspected from his growing intolerance and bitterness that the Americans were gaining unexpected advantages. But she knew nothing of what was happening. She could hear from afar off the marching and movements of soldiers, the blare of military music, and the faint echoes of hurrahing multitudes, but there was no one to give her any certain information. Still, she guessed something from the anger of the priest and the reticence of the Mexican servants. If good fortune had been with Santa Anna, she was sure she would have heard of "The glorious! The invincible! The magnificent Presidente de la Republica Mexicana! The Napoleon of the West!"

It was not permitted her to go into the city. A proposal to do so had been met with a storm of angry amazement. Steam and electricity had not then annihilated distance and abolished suspense. She could but wonder and hope and try to read the truth from a covert inspection of the face and words of Fray Ignatius.

---

[30]rebozo—a long shawl worn over the head and shoulders

Between this monk and herself the breach was hourly
widening. With angry pain she saw her mother tortured
between the fact that she loved her husband, and the
horrible doubt that to love him was a mortal sin. She
understood the underlying motive which prompted the
priest to urge upon the Señora the removal of herself and
her daughters to the convent. His offer to take charge of
the Worth residencia and estate was in her conviction a
proposal to rob them of all rights in it. She felt certain
that whatever the Church once grasped in its iron hand,
it would ever retain. And both to Isabel and herself the
thought of a convent was now horrible. "They will force
me to be a nun," said Isabel, "and then, what will Luis
do? And they will never tell me anything about my
father and my brothers. I should never hear of them. I
should never see them any more; unless the good God
was so kind as to let me meet them in His heaven."

Antonia had still darker and more fearful thoughts.
She had not forgotten the stories whispered to her in
childhood of the dreadful fates reserved for contuma-
cious and disobedient women. Whenever Fray Ignatius
looked at her she felt as if she were within the shadow of
the Inquisition.

Never had days passed so wearily and anxiously.
Never had nights been so terrible. The sisters did not
dare to talk much together; they doubted Rachela, and
they were sure their words were listened to and repeated.
They were not permitted to be alone with the Señora.
Fray Ignatius had particularly warned Rachela to prevent
this. He was gradually bringing the unhappy woman
into what he called "a heavenly mind"—the influence of

her daughters, he was sure, would be that of worldly
affections and sinful liberty. Rachela obeyed the confessor so faithfully, that the Señora was almost in a state of
solitary confinement. Every day her will was growing
weaker, her pathetic obedience more childlike and
absolute.

But at midnight, when every one was asleep, Antonia
stepped softly into her sister's room and talked to her.
They sat on Isabel's bed clasping each other's hand in the
dark, and speaking in whispers. Then Antonia warned
and strengthened Isabel. She told her all her fears. She
persuaded her to control her wilfulness, to be obedient,
and to assume the childlike thoughtlessness which best
satisfied Fray Ignatius. "He told you to-day to be happy,
that he would think for you. Let him believe that is the
thing you want," said Antonia. "I assure you we shall be
the safer for it."

"He said to me yesterday, when I asked him about the
war, 'Do not inquire, child, into things you do not understand. That is to be irreligious,' and then he made the
cross on his breast, as if I had put a bad thought into his
heart. We are afraid all day, and we sit whispering all
night about our fears; that is the state we are in. The
Lord sends us nothing but misfortunes, Antonia."

"My darling, tell the Lord your sorrow, then, but do
not repine to Rachela or Fray Ignatius. That is to com-
plain to the merciless of the All-Merciful."

"Do you think I am wicked, Antonia? What excuse
could I offer to His Divine Majesty, if I spoke evil to Him
of Rachela and Fray Ignatius?"

"Neither of them are our friends; do you think so?"

"Fray Ignatius looks like a goblin; he gives me a shiver when he looks at me. And as for Rachela—I already hate her!"

"Do not trust her. You need not hate her, Isabel."

In conversations like these the anxious girls passed the long, and often very cold, nights. The days were still worse, for as November went slowly away the circumstances which surrounded their lives appeared to constantly gather a more decided and bitter tone. December, usually a month of happiness bright with Christmas expectations and Christmas joys, came in with a terribly severe, wet norther. The great log fires only warmed the atmosphere immediately surrounding them, and Isabel and Antonia sat gloomily within it all day. It seemed to Antonia as if her heart had come to the very end of hope—that something must happen.

The rain lashed the earth; the wind roared around the house, filling it with unusual noises. The cold was a torture that few found themselves able to endure. But it brought a compensation. Fray Ignatius did not leave the Mission comforts, and Rachela could not bear to go prowling about the corridors and passages. She established herself in the Señora's room and remained there. And very early in the evening she said she had "an outrageous headache" and went to her room.

Then Antonia and Isabel sat awhile by their mother's bed. They talked in whispers of their father and brothers, and when the Señora cried, they kissed her sobs into silence and wiped her tears away. In that hour, if Fray Ignatius had known it, they undid, in a great measure, the work to which he had given more than a month of patient and deeply reflective labor. For with the girls, there was the wondrous charm of love and nature; but with the priest, only a splendid ideal of a Church universal that was to swallow up all the claims of love and ties of nature.

It was nearly nine o'clock when Antonia and Isabel returned to the parlor fire. Their hearts were full of sorrow for their mother and of fears for their own future, for this confidence had shown them how firmly the refuge of the convent had been planted in the anxious ideas of the Señora. Fortunately, the cold had driven the servants either to the kitchen fire or to their beds, and the sisters could talk over the subject without fear of interference.

"Are you sleepy, queridita?"

"I think I shall never go to sleep again, Antonia. If I shut my eyes I shall find myself in the convent, and I do not want to go there even in a dream. Do you know Mother Teresa? Well then, I could tell you things. She does not like me, I am sure of that—quite sure."

"I am going to make us a cup of tea. It will do us good."

"If indeed it were chocolate!"

"I cannot make chocolate now; but you shall have a great deal of sugar in your cup, and something good to eat also. Put your chair close to the fire, and we will sit here until we are quite sleepy."

With the words she went into the kitchen. Molly was nodding over her beads, in the comfortable radius made by the blazing logs; no one else was present but a young peasant. He brought a small kettle to the parlor fire, lifted a table to the hearth, and then replenished the pile of logs for burning during the night. Isabel, cuddling in a large chair, watched Antonia, as she went softly about putting on the table such delicacies as she could find at that hour. Tamales and cold duck, sweet cake and the guava jelly that was Isabel's favorite dainty. There was a little comfort in the sight of these things, and also in the bright silver teapot standing so cheerfully on the hearth, diffusing through the room its warm, soothing perfume.

"I think I shall like that American tea tonight, Antonia, but you must half fill my cup with those little blocks of sugar—quite half fill it, Antonia. Have you found cream? Then a great deal of cream."

Antonia stood still a moment and looked at the drowsy little beauty. Her eyes were closed, and her head nestled comfortably in a corner of the padded chair. Then a hand upon the door-handle arrested her attention, and Antonia turned her eyes from Isabel to see Ortiz, the peasant, peer into the room and then disappear. Don Luis entered swiftly after him, and before anyone could say a word he was kneeling beside Isabel.

Antonia looked with amazement and delight at this apparition. How had he come? She put her hand upon his sleeve; it was scarcely wet. His dress was splendid; if he had been going to a tertulia[31] of the highest class, he could not have been more richly adorned. And the storm was yet raging! It was a miracle.

"Dear Luis, sit down! Here is a chair close to Iza! I will go for mi madre. O yes! She will come! You shall see, Iza! And then, Luis, we shall have some supper."

_____

[31]tertulia [tĕr·tōōl′yä]—an evening party

Antonia was not a minute in reaching her mother's room. The unhappy lady was half-lying among the large pillows of her gilded bed, wide awake. Her black eyes were fixed upon a crucifix at its foot, and she was slowly murmuring prayers upon her rosary.

"Madre! Madre! Luis is here, Luis is here! Come quick, mi madre. Here are your stockings and slippers, and your gown, and your mantilla—no, no, no, do not call Rachela. Luis has news of my father and of Jack! Oh, madre, he has a letter from Jack to you! Come dear, come, in a few minutes you will be ready."

She was gently urging the trembling woman and dressing her in spite of her faint effort to delay—to call Rachela—to bring Luis to her room. In ten minutes she was ready. She went down softly, like a frightened child, Antonia cheering and encouraging her in whispers.

When she entered the cheerful parlor the shadow of a smile flitted over her wan face. Luis ran to meet her. He drew the couch close to the hearth; he helped Antonia arrange her comfortably upon it. He made her tea, and kissed her hands when he put it into them. And then Isabel made Luis a cup, and cut his tamales, and waited upon him with such pretty service that the happy suitor thought he was eating a meal in Paradise.

For a few minutes it had been only this ordinary gladness of reunion; but it was impossible to ignore longer the anxiety in the eyes that asked him so many questions. He took two letters from his pockets and gave them to the Señora. They were from her husband and Jack. Her hands trembled; she kissed them fervently; and as she placed them to her breast the tears dropped down upon them.

Antonia opened the real conversation with that never-failing wedge, the weather. "You came through the storm, Luis? Yet you are scarcely wet. Now then, explain this miracle."

"I went first to Lopez Navarro's. Do you not know this fiesta dress? It is the one Lopez bought for the feast of St. James. He lent it to me, for I assure you that my own clothing was like that of a beggar man. It was impossible that I could see my angel on earth in it."

"But in such weather? You cannot have come far to-day?"

"Señorita, there are things which are impossible, quite impossible! That is one of them. Early this morning the north wind advanced upon us, sword in hand. But it was absolutely necessary that someone should reach San Antonio tonight, and I was so happy as to persuade General Burleson to send me."

"Have you seen the Señor Doctor lately, Luis?" asked the Señora.

"I left him at nightfall."

"At nightfall! But that is impossible!"

"It is true. The army of the Americans is but a few miles from San Antonio."

"Luis!"

"Did you not know, Señora?"

"We know nothing but what Fray Ignatius tells us— that the Americans have been everywhere pulling down churches, and granting martyrdom to the priests, and that everywhere miraculous retributions have pursued them."

"Was Gonzales a retribution? The Señor Doctor came to us while we were there. God be blessed—he startled us like the rattle of rifle-shots in the midnight! 'Why were you not at Goliad?' he cried. 'There were three hundred stand of arms there, and cannon, and plenty of provisions. Why were they not yours?' You would have thought, Señora, he had been a soldier all his life. The men caught fire when he came near them, and we went to Goliad like eagles flying for their prey. We took the town, and the garrison, and all the arms and military stores. I will tell you something that came to pass there. At midnight, as Jack and I stood with the Señor Doctor by the camp-fire, a stranger rode up to us. It was Colonel Milam. He was flying from a Mexican prison and had not yet heard of the revolt. He made the camp ring with his shout of delight. He was impatient for the morning. He was the first man who entered the garrison. Bravissimo! What a soldier is he!"

"I remember him!" cried the Señora. "Mi Roberto brought him here once. So splendid a man I never saw before. So tall, so handsome, so gallant, so like a hero. He is an American from—well, then, I have forgotten the place."

"From Kentucky. He fought with the Mexicans when they were fighting for their liberty; but when they wanted a king and a dictator he resigned his commission and was thrown into prison. He has a long bill against Santa Anna."

"We must not forget, Luis," said the Señora with a little flash of her old temper, "that Santa Anna represents to good Catholics the triumph of Holy Church."

Luis devoutly crossed himself. "I am her dutiful son, I assure you, Señora—always."

A warning glance from Antonia changed the conversation. There was plenty to tell which touched them mainly on the side of the family, and the Señora listened, with pride which she could not conceal, to the exploits of her husband and sons, though she did not permit herself to confess the feeling. And her heart softened to her children. Without acknowledging the tie between Isabel and Luis, she permitted or was oblivious to the favors it allowed.

Certainly many little formalities could be dispensed with, in a meeting so unexpected and so eventful. When the pleasant impromptu meal was over, even the Señora had eaten and drunk with enjoyment. Then Luis set the table behind them, and they drew closer to the fire. At the dark, cold midnight they found an hour or two of sweetest consolation. It was indeed hard to weary these three heart-starved women; they asked question after question, and when any brought out the comical side of camp life, they forgot their pleasure was almost a clandestine one and laughed outright.

In the very midst of such a laugh, Rachela entered the room. She stood in speechless amazement, gazing with a dark, malicious face upon the happy group. "Señorita Isabel!" she screamed. "But this is abominable! At the midnight also! Who could have believed in such wickedness? Grace of Mary, it is inconceivable!"

She laid her hand roughly on Isabel's shoulder, and Luis removed it with as little courtesy. "You were not called," he said, with the haughty insolence of a Mexican noble to a servant. "Depart."

"My Señora! Listen! You yourself also—you will die. You that are so weak—so broken-hearted—"

Then a miracle occurred. The Señora threw off the nightmare of selfish sorrow and spiritual sentimentality which had held her in bondage. With a scornful air, she repeated the words of Luis:

"You were not called. Depart."

"The Señorita Isabel?"

"Is in my care. Her mother's care! Do you understand?"

"My Señora, Fray Ignatius—"

"Saints in heaven! But this is intolerable! Go."

Then Rachela closed the door with a clang which echoed through the house. It was impossible after this interruption to recall the happy spirit dismissed by it, and Rachela had the consolation, as she muttered beside the fire in the Señora's room, of this conviction. So when she heard the party breaking up half an hour afterwards, she complimented herself upon her influence.

"Will Jack come and see me soon, and the Senor Doctor?" questioned the Señora, anxiously, as she held the hand of Luis in parting.

"Jack is on a secret message to General Houston. His return will find us, I trust, in San Antonio. But until we have taken the city, no American can safely enter it. For this reason, when it was necessary to give Lopez Navarro certain instructions, I volunteered to bring them. I have had my reward," he said, lifting the Señora's hand and kissing it.

"But, then, even you are in danger."

"Si! If I am discovered; but, blessed be the hand of God! Luis Alveda knows where he is going, and how to get there."

"I have heard," said the Señora in a hushed voice, "that there are to be no prisoners. That is Santa Anna's order."

"I heard it twenty days ago, and am still suffocating over it."

"Ah, Luis, you do not know the man yet! I heard Fray Ignatius say that."

"We know him well, and also what he is capable of." And Luis plucked his mustache fiercely, as he bowed a silent farewell to the ladies.

They went very quietly upstairs. The Señora was anticipating the interview she expected with Rachela, and, perhaps wisely, she isolated herself in an atmosphere of sullen and haughty silence. She would accept nothing from her, not even sympathy or flattery. In a curt dismissal, she managed to make her attendant feel the immeasurable distance between a high-born lady of the house of Flores and a poor beggar that she had taken from the streets of Madrid. Rachela knew the Señora was thinking of this circumstance; the thought was in her voice, and it cowed and snubbed the woman, her nature being essentially as low as her birth.

As for the Señora, the experience did her a world of good. She waited upon herself as a princess might condescend to minister to her own wants—loftily, with a smile at her own complaisance. The very knowledge that her husband was near at hand inspired her with courage.

She went to sleep assuring herself "that not even Fray Ignatius should again speak evil of her beloved, who never thought of her except with a loyal affection." For in married life, the wife can sin against love as well as fidelity, and she thought with a sob of the cowardice which had permitted Fray Ignatius to call her dear one "rebel and heretic."

"It is not a mortal sin to think differently from Santa Anna," she said in a passionate whisper.

And if Fray Ignatius had seen at that moment the savage whiteness of her small teeth behind the petulant pout of her parted lips, he might have understood that this woman of small intelligence had also the unreasoning partisanship and the implacable sense of anger which generally accompanies small intelligence, and which indicates a nature governed by feeling, and utterly irresponsive to reasoning which feeling does not endorse.

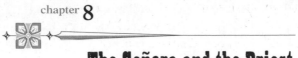

chapter 8

The Señora and the Priest

*I*t was nearly two o'clock when Don Luis mounted his horse and left the Worth residencia. The storm still raged, the night was dark, and the cold intense; but the home of Lopez Navarro was scarce a quarter of a mile away, and Luis found him waiting his return.

"You have still an hour, Luis. Come in and sit with me."

"As you say. I wish to show you that I am capable of a great thing. You do not believe me? Well, then give me again my own clothes. I will resign these."

"You are most welcome to them, Luis."

"But no, I am in earnest. The fight is at hand—they are too fine."

"Yes, but I tell you—there is to be a grand day for freedom; well, then, for a fiesta one puts on the best that is to be got. I will even lend you my Cross of Saint James, if you wish. A young hero should be dressed like a hero. Honor my poor clothes so far as to wear them in the fight."

"Thank you, Lopez. I will not disgrace them."

"Listen to me, Luis. As a matter of precision, where now are the Americans?"

"At the mission of Espada."

"La Espada?—the sword—the name is ominous."

"Of success, Lopez."

"Is Houston, then, with you?"

"Until a few days ago. He and General Austin have gone to San Felipe."

"For what? Is not San Antonio the most important point?"

"It was decided by the vote of the army to send them there to frame a provisional government. There are plenty of fighters with us, but not one statesman like Houston. And now it is necessary that we should have legal authority to obtain loans, maintain the army in the field, and many other such things vital to our cause. Austin is to go to the United States. He will bring back men and money. Houston must draw up our declaration and manifestoes; direct the civil government; forward troops; and, in fact, set a new government in motion."

"He is the loadstone[32] in the bosom! I wonder that the Americans permitted that he should leave them."

"He, and he only, was the man to go. Ere he left, he said some strange words. I shall not, as a Mexican, forget them.

"He said, 'You will fight as men fight for their homes, and their wives, and their children, but also—remember this—the idea of Texas is in the American heart! Two generations they have carried it there! It is your destiny to make the idea a fact! As far back as 1819, Adams wanted Texas. When Adams became president, he told

---

[32]loadstone—charm against evil

Poinsett to offer Mexico a million dollars for Texas. Clay
would have voted three million. Van Buren, in 1829, told
Poinsett to offer five million for Texas. I went to Washington that year, and proposed to revolutionize Texas. I
declare to you that the highest men in the land were of my
mind. Only last July President Jackson offered an addi-
tional half million dollars for the Rio Grande boundary,
and Mr. Secretary Forsyth said that one way or another
Texas must become part of our country. We have been
longing for it for fifty years! Now, then, brothers-in-arms!'
he cried, 'You are here for your homes and your freedom;
but, more than that, you are here for your country!'
Remember the thousands of Americans who have bought
this land with their blood! We have held a grip on Texas
for fifty years. By the soul of every American who has
perished here, I charge you, No Surrender!' "

"You should have heard the shout that answered the
charge. It made my heart leap to my bosom. And ever
since, the two words have filled the air. You could see
men catching them on their lips. They are in their eyes,
and their walk. Their hands say them. The up-toss of
their heads says them. When they go into battle they will
see Houston in front of them, and hear him call back 'No
surrender!' Mexico cannot hold Texas against such a
determined purpose, carried out by such determined
men."

Lopez did not answer. He was a melancholy, well-read
man, who had traveled and to whom the idea of liberty
was a passion. But the feeling of race was also strong in
him, and he could not help regretting that liberty must
come to Texas through an alien people. It brought others

equally living to him, and he asked, "Where, then, is Doctor Worth?"

"At Espada. The army wished him to go to San Felipe with Houston, but he declined. And we want him most of all, both as a fighter and a physician. His son Thomas went in his place."

"I know not Thomas."

"Indeed, very few know him. He is one that seldom speaks. But his rifle has its word always ready."

"And Jack?"

"Jack also went to San Felipe. He is to bring back the first despatches. Jack is the favorite of the camp. Ah, what a happy soul he has! One would think that it had just come from heaven, or was just going there."

"Did you see Señorita Antonia tonight?"

"Si! She is a blessing to the eyesight. So brave a young girl, so sweet, so wise; she is a miracle! If I loved not Isabel with my whole soul, I would kneel at Antonia's feet."

"That is where I also would kneel."

"How the wind roars and the rain beats the house! But our men have the shelter of one of the panchos. You should have heard the padre threaten them with the anger of heaven and hell and General Cos. Good-bye, Lopez. I have stayed my last moment now."

"Your horse has been well fed. Listen, he is neighing for you. To Doctor Worth give my honorable regards. Is Señor Parades with you? and Perez Mexia? Say to them I keep the vow I made in their behalf. Farewell, Luis!"

It was just dawn when Luis reached camp and found Doctor Worth waiting his arrival. Fortunately there was nothing but good news for the doctor. Luis had seen everything through the medium of his own happiness, and he described the midnight meal and the Señora's amiability with the utmost freedom from anything unpleasant. Rachela's interference he treated with scornful indifference; yet it affected Worth's mind unpleasantly. For it went straight to the source of offence. "She must have had Fray Ignatius behind her. And my poor Maria, she will be as dough for them to knead as they desire to!"

In fact, as he was thus thinking, the Señora was lying awake in her bed, anticipating her confessor's next visit. She was almost glad the norther was still blowing. It would give her another day's respite. "And so many things happen as the clock goes round," she reflected. Perhaps even her Roberto might arrive; it would not be more wonderful than the visit of Luis Alveda.

But very early in the day she saw the father hurrying up the oleander avenue. The wind tossed his gown and blew his hat backward and sideways, compelling him to make undignified haste. How such little things affect the mental poise and mood! The Senora smiled at the funny figure he made, and with the smile came a feeling of resistance to his tyranny and a stubborn determination to defend her own conduct.

He came into her room with a doleful countenance, saying, as he crossed himself, "God be here!"

"And with you, father," answered the Señora, cheerfully—a mood she had assumed at the last moment, by a kind of instinct.

"There is evil news on every hand, my daughter. The heretics are swarming like wolves around the Missions.

Several of our holy brothers have endured the last extremity. These wolves will even enter the city, and you
will be in danger. I have come to take you to the convent.
There, Holy Mary will be your safety."

"But these wolves might attack the convent, father!"

"Our Blessed Lady is stronger than they. She has
always kept her own."

"Ah, Antonia! Listen to Fray Ignatius! He says we
must go to the convent—the heretics are coming. They
have even slain some priests at the Mission."

"Fray Ignatius has been misinformed, dear mother.
When a man wears a gown and is unarmed, Americans
do not molest him. That is certain. As for the convent, it
is impossible. My father forbade it. If the Americans
enter the city, he is with them. He will protect us, if we
should need it, which is not likely."

"Disobedient one!"

"Pardon. I wish only to obey the commands of my
father."

"I absolve you from them."

"They are between God and my soul. There is no
absolution from duty."

"Hear you, Señora! Hear you the rebellious and
disobedient one! She has defied me to my face! She is
near to being anathema! She is not your daughter! She
is bewitched. Some evil spirit has possession of her. Let
no one touch her or speak to her; it shall be a mortal sin."

Antonia fell at her mother's knee. "Mi madre! I am
your daughter, your Antonia, that loves you better than
life. Permit me not to be accused of sin—to be called a
devil. Mother, speak for me."

At this moment Isabel entered. Seeing the distress of her mother and sister she hastened to them, but Fray Ignatius stepped between, and extending his arms forbade her nearer approach.

"I forbid you to speak to your sister. I forbid you to touch her, to give her food, or water, or sympathy, until she has humbled herself, and obtained the forgiveness of her sin."

Then mother love stood up triumphant over superstition. "I and my daughter are the same," said the Señora, and she gave her hand to Antonia. "If she has sinned, we will bear the penance together, she and I together."

"I command you to stand apart. For the good of Antonia's sinful soul, I command you to withdraw yourself from her."

"She is my daughter, father. I will bear the sin and the punishment with her. The Holy Mother will understand me. To her I will go."

The door of her room was at hand. She stepped swiftly to it, and putting her daughters before her, passed in and turned the key.

The movement took the priest by surprise, and yet he was secretly satisfied with it. He had permitted himself to act with an imprudence most unusual. He had allowed the Señora to find out her own moral strength, and had made a situation for her in which she had acted not only without his support but against his authority.

"And yet," he muttered, "so much depends upon my persuading her into the convent; however, nothing now is to be done today, except to see Rachela. Saint Joseph! if these American heretics were only in my power! What a long joy I would make of them! I would cut a throat—just one throat—every day of my life."

The hatred which could contemplate a vengeance so long drawn out was on his dark face; yet it is but justice to say that he sincerely believed it to be a holy hatred. The foes of the Church, he regarded as the foes of God, and his anger he considered a just zeal. Beside which, he had a far more tangible cause.

The accumulated treasures of the Missions—their gold and gems, their costly vestments and holy vessels—had been removed to the convent for safety. "These infidels of Americans give to women the honor they should give to God and Holy Church," he said to his brethren. "They will not suffer the Sisters to be molested; and our wealth will be safe wherever they are."

But this wealth was really so immense that he believed it might be well to secure it still further, and knowing the position Dr. Worth held among his countrymen, he resolved to induce the man's wife and daughters to seek refuge within the convent. They were, in fact, to be held as hostages, for the protection of the property of the Church.

That he should fail in his plan was intolerable to him. He had been so confident of success. He imagined the smile on the face of Fray Sarapiam, and the warning against self-confidence he would receive from his superior. He vowed by Saint Joseph that he would not suffer himself to be so mortified by three women.

Had he seen the Señora after the first excitement of her rebellion was over, he would have been satisfied of the validity of his authority, at least as regarded her. She flung herself at the foot of her altar, weeping and beating her breast in a passion of self-accusation and contrition. Certainly, she had stood by her daughter in the presence of the priest; but in her room she withdrew herself from the poor girl as if she were a spiritual leper.

Antonia at a distance watched the self-abasement of her mother. She could not weep, but she was white as clay, and her heart was swollen with a sense of wrong and injustice, until breathing was almost suffocation. She looked with a piteous entreaty at Isabel. Her little sister had taken a seat at the extremity of the room away from her. She watched Antonia with eyes full of terror. But there was no sympathy in her face, only an uncertainty which seemed to speak to her—to touch her— and her mother was broken-hearted with shame and grief.

The anxiety was also a dumb one. Until the Señora rose from her knees, there was not a movement made, not a word uttered. The girls waited shivering with cold, sick with fear, until she spoke. Even then her words were cold as the wind outside:

"Go to your room, Antonia. You have not only sinned; you have made me sin also."

"Mi madre, I am innocent of wrong. I have committed no sin. Is it a sin to obey my father? Isabel, darling, speak for me."

"But, then, what have you done, Antonia?"

"Fray Ignatius wants us to go to the convent. I refused. My father made me promise to do so. Is not our first duty to our father? Mother, is it not?

"No, no. It is to God—and to Fray Ignatius, as the priest of God. He says we ought to go to the convent. He knows best. We have been disobedient and wicked."

"Isabel, speak. Tell mi madre if you think we should go."

There was a moment's wavering, and then Isabel went to her mother and caressed her as only Isabel could, and with a kiss she said boldly: "Mi madre, we will not go to the convent. Not any of us. It is a dreadful place, even for a happy child."

"Hush, child! I cannot listen to you! Go away! I must be alone. I must think. I must pray. Only the Mother of Sorrows can help me."

It was a miserable sequel to the happy night, and Antonia was really terrified at the position in which she found herself. If the Americans should fail, nothing but flight, or uncompromising submission to Fray Ignatius, remained for her. She knew only too well how miserable her life could be made—what moral torture could be inflicted—what spiritual servitude exacted. In a moment of time she had comprehended her danger, and her heart sank and sickened with a genuine physical terror.

The cold was still severe, and no one answered her call for wood. Isabel crouched, white and shivering, over the dying embers, and it was she who first uttered the fear Antonia had refused to admit to herself—"Suppose the servants are forbidden to wait upon us!"

"I will bring wood myself, dearest." She was greatly comforted by the word "us." She could almost have wept for joy of the sympathy it included. For thought is rapid in such crucial moments, and she had decided that even flight with her would be a kinder fate for Isabel than the cruel tender mercies of the Sisters and the convent.

They could not talk much. The thought of their mother's anguish, and of the separation put between them and their household, shocked and terrified them. Vainly they called for fuel. At dinner time no table was laid, and no preparations made for the meal. The Señora had evidently not been included in the ban, for Rachela attended with ostentatious care to her comfort.

Antonia went into the kitchen with some food and cooked it. She brought wood into the parlor, and made up the fire. Fortunately, her northern education had given her plenty of resources for such emergencies. Two or three savory dishes were soon ready, and the small table set upon a warm, bright hearth.

Isabel had rolled herself up in a wadded silk coverlet and gone to sleep. Antonia awakened her with a kiss. "Come, queridita, and get your dinner."

"But is it possible? I thought Fray Ignatius had forbidden it."

"He cannot forbid me to wait upon you, darling, and he cannot turn the flour into dust or the meat into stone. There is a good dinner ready, and you are hungry, no doubt."

"For three hours I have been faint. Ah! you have made me a custard also! You are a very comforter."

But the girl was still and sad, and Antonia was hard pressed to find any real comfort for her. For she knew that their only hope lay in the immediate attack of the American force and its success, and she did not think it wise to hide from her sister the alternatives that lay before them if the Americans failed.

"I am afraid," said Isabel, "and so unhappy. A very sad business is life. I cannot think how any one can care to live."

"Remember Luis, and our father, and Jack, and Thomas, and our dear mother, who this morning stood between us and Fray Ignatius. Will you let this priest turn the sky black above you?"

Fortunately, the norther moderated at sunset. Life then seemed so much more possible. Adverse elements intensify adverse fortune, and the physical suffering from the cold had also benumbed Antonia's spirits and made her less hopeful and less clear-visioned. But when she awoke at the gray dawn of the next day, she awoke with a different spirit. She had regained herself. She rose quietly, and looked out towards the city. The black flag from the Alamo and the Missions hung above it. She looked at the ominous standards, and then the tears sprang to her eyes; she lifted her face to heaven, and a few words, swifter than light, sprang from her soul into the ear of the Eternal Father of Spirits.

The answer came with the petition—came with the crack of rifle shots; precise, regular, unceasing.

"O God I thank Thee! Lord of Hosts, Thou art a great multitude! Isabel! Isabel! The Americans are attacking the city! Our father will fight his way back to his home! Fray Ignatius cannot come today. Listen! How the Mexicans are shouting! They are cheering on the men. What a turmoil!"

"Jesu, Maria, have mercy!" cried Isabel, clasping her crucifix and falling upon her knees.

"Oh, Isabel, pray for our father."

"And Luis?"

"And Luis, and Thomas, and Jack, and Dare. There are prayers for them all, and love enough to make them. Hear the drums, and the trumpets, and the gallop of the cavalry. Come, let us go to our mother. Today, no one will remember Fray Ignatius."

chapter 9

The Storming of the Alamo

*T*he Señora was already dressed. She turned with a face full of fear and anger to her daughters as they entered her room—

"These American diablos! They are attacking the city. They will take it—that is to be expected—who can fight diablos? And what is to become of us? Oh, Antonia! Why did you prevent Fray Ignatius? We might now have been safe in the convent," and Rachela nodded her head in assent, with an insufferable air of reproof and toleration.

Antonia saw that the time had not yet come for pleading her own cause. She left Isabel with her mother. The Señora's breakfast was waiting, and she offered to share it with her youngest daughter. Antonia went downstairs to prepare for herself some coffee. She was surprised and pleased to find it made. For a certain thought had come to Molly in the night and she had acted upon it—

"The praist is a strange praist, and I'd be a poor body, I think, to let him be meddling wid my work. Shure, I never heard of the like of such interfering in Ireland, nor in the States at all!" Then turning to the Mexican cook, Manuel—"You may lave the fire alone till I bees done wid it."

"Fray Ignatius will not give you absolution if you disobey him."

"He can be kaping the same then. There is an Irish praist at San Patricio, and I'll be going there for my absolution. I'll be getting none any nearer that an Irish soul will be a pin the better for. I'll say that, standing in the church, to the saints themselves. So be aff wid you and let the fire alone till I bees done wid it."

But it was not Molly's place to serve the food she cooked, and she did not trouble herself about the serving. When she had asserted her right to control her own work, and do it or neglect it as she pleased, she was satisfied. Over Antonia—who was at least half a Mexican—she acknowledged a Mexican priest to have authority, and she had no intention of interfering between Fray Ignatius and his lawful flock. She was smoking her pipe by the fire when Antonia entered the kitchen, and she neither lifted her eyes nor spoke to her.

Against such unreasonable isolation Antonia could not help a feeling of anger, and she heard with satisfaction the regular crack of the rifles. Her thought was—"They will make these people find their tongues also, very soon." As she ate her roll and drank her coffee, she considered how they might gain news of the battle. For even if Fray Ignatius were able to visit them, his report would be colored by his prejudices and his desires, and could not be relied on.

Her heart fluttered and sank; she was hot and cold, sanguine and fearful. She could not endure the idea of a suspense unrelieved by any reliable word. The siege might be a long one. San Antonio was strongly walled and well defended. The Alamo fortress stood in its center; it had forty-eight cannon and a garrison of a thousand men; and before it could be reached, the city had to be taken.

As soon as she was alone with her mother, she pointed out these facts to her. "Let me write to Lopez Navarro, mi madre. He is a friend."

"Of the Americans! Si."

"Of freedom. He will send us word."

"Are you forgetful of what is moral and respectable, Antonia? That a young lady should write to Lopez Navarro—a man that is unmarried—is such a thing as never before happened! He would think the world had come to an end, or worse."

"Dear mother! In a time of trouble like this, who would think wrong of us? Surely you might write."

"As you say, Antonia. Tell me, then, who will take the letter."

"The peasant Ortiz will take it. This morning he brought in wood and kindled the fire, and I saw in his face the kindness of his heart."

After some further persuasion, the Señora agreed to

write, and Ortiz undertook the commission with a nod of understanding. There remained nothing to be done but to listen and to watch. Fortunately, however, Rachela found the center of interest among the servants in the kitchen, leaving the Señora and her daughter free to converse without espionage.

Just after sunset a letter arrived from Navarro. Rachela lingered in the room to learn its contents. But the Señora, having read them, passed the letter to Antonia and Isabel. Rachela watched with anger as Antonia, having carefully considered the letter, threw it into the fire. The news it brought was not unfavorable:

"SENORA MARIA FLORES WORTH:

"I send this on December the fifth, in the year of our Blessed Lord and Lady 1835. It is my honor and pleasure to tell you that the Americans, having performed miracles of valor, reached the Plaza this afternoon. Here the main body of the Mexican troops received them, and there has been severe fighting. At sunset, the Mexicans retreated within the Alamo. The Texans have taken possession of the Veramendi House, and the portion of the city surrounding it. There has been a great slaughter of our poor countrymen. I charge myself whenever I pass the Plaza, to say a paternoster for the souls who fell there. Señora Maria Flores Worth, I kiss your hands. I kiss also the hands of the Señorita Antonia, and the hands of the Señorita Isabel, and I make haste to sign myself,

"Your servant,

"LOPEZ NAVARRO."

This little confidence between mother and daughters restored the tone of feeling between them. They had something to talk of, personal and exclusive. In the fear and uncertainty, they forgot priestly interdiction and clung to each other with that affection which is the strength of danger and the comforter of sorrow.

On the following day the depression deepened. The sounds of battle were closer at hand. The Mexican servants had an air of insolence and triumph. Antonia feared for the evening's report—if indeed Navarro should be able to send one. She feared more when she saw the messenger early in the afternoon. "Too early is often worse than too late." The proverb shivered upon her trembling lips as she took the letter from him. The three women read it together, with sinking hearts:

"SENORA MARIA FLORES WORTH:

"This on the sixth of December, in the year of our Blessed Lord and Lady 1835. The brave, the illustrious Colonel Milam is dead. I watched him three hours in to-day's fight. A man so calm was inconceivable. He was smiling when the ball struck him—when he fell. The Texans, after his loss, retired to their quarters. This was at the hour of eleven. At the hour of one, the Mexicans made another sortie from the Alamo. The Texans rushed to meet them with an incredible vengeance. Their leader was General Burleson. He showed himself to General Cos in a sheet of flame. Such men are not to be fought. General Cos was compelled to retire to the Alamo. The battle is over for to-day. On this earth the soul has but a mortal sword. The water in the river is red with blood. The Plaza is covered with the dead and the dying. I have the honor to tell you that these 'miserables' are being attended to by the noble, the charitable Señor Doctor Worth. As I write, he is kneeling among them. My soul adores his humanity. I humbly kiss your hands, Señora, and the hands of your exalted daughters.

"LOPEZ NAVARRO."

Until midnight this letter furnished the anxious, loving women with an unceasing topic of interest. The allusion to her husband made the Señora weep. She retired to her oratory and poured out her love and her fears in holy salutations, in thanksgivings and entreaties.

The next morning there was an ominous lull in the atmosphere. As men run backward to take a longer leap forward, so both armies were taking breath for a fiercer struggle. In the Worth residencia, the suspense was becoming hourly harder to endure. The Señora and her daughters were hardly conscious of the home life around them. It mattered little to them now whether food was cooked or not. They were neither hungry nor sleepy. Existence was prayer and expectation.

Just before sunset Antonia saw Don Lopez coming through the garden. The Señora, accompanied by her daughters, went to meet him. His face was perplexed and troubled:

"General Cos has been joined by Ugartechea with three hundred men," he said. "You will see now that the fight will be still more determined."

Before daylight broke on the morning of the 5th, the Americans attacked the Alamo. The black flag waved above them, and the city itself had the stillness of death, but for hours the dull roar and the clamorous tumult went on without cessation. The Señora lay upon her bed motionless, with hands tightly locked. She had exhausted feeling and was passive. Antonia and Isabel wandered from window to window, hoping to see some token which would indicate the course of events.

Nothing was visible but the ferocious flag flying out above the desperate men fighting below it. So black! So cruel and defiant it looked! It seemed to darken and fill the whole atmosphere around it. And though the poor women had not dared to whisper to each other what it said to them, they knew in their own hearts that it meant, if the Americans failed, the instant and brutal massacre of every prisoner.

The husband and father were under its inhuman shadow. So most probably were Darius Grant and Luis Alveda. It was even likely that Jack might have returned ere the fight, and was with the besiegers. Every time they went to the window, it filled their hearts with horror.

In the middle of the afternoon it suddenly disappeared. Antonia watched breathlessly. Several times before, it had been dropped by some American rifle, but this time it was not as speedily replaced. In a few minutes she uttered a shrill cry. It was in a voice so strained, so piercing, so unlike her own, that the Señora leaped from her bed. Antonia turned to meet her mother with white, parted lips. She was speechless with excess of feeling, but she pointed to the Alamo. The black flag was no longer there! A white one was flying in its place.

"IT IS A SURRENDER!" gasped Antonia. "IT IS A SURRENDER!" As if in response to her words, a mighty shout and a simultaneous salute of rifles hailed the emblem of victory.

An hour afterwards, a little Mexican boy came running with all his speed. He brought a few lines from Don Lopez. They had evidently been written in a great hurry on a piece of paper torn from his pocket-book, but how welcome they were. The very lack of formality gave to them a certain hurry of good fortune:

> "May you and yours be God's care for many years to come, Señora! The Mexicans have surrendered the Alamo, and asked for quarter. These noble-minded Americans have given it. The Señor Doctor will bring you good news. I rejoice with you.
>
> "LOPEZ NAVARRO."

Death and captivity had been turned away from their home, and the first impulse of these pious, simple-hearted women was a prayer of thanksgiving. Then Antonia remembered the uncomfortable state of the household and the probable necessities of the men coming back from mortal strife and the shadow of death.

She found that the news had already changed the domestic atmosphere. Every servant was attending to his duty. Everyone professed a great joy in the expected arrival of the Señor. And what a happy impetus the hope gave to her own hands! How delightful it was to be once more arranging the evening meal and brightening the rooms with fire and light!

Soon after dark they heard the swing of the garden gate, the tramp of rapid footsteps, and the high-pitched voices of excited men. The door was flung open wide. The Señora forgot that it was cold. She went with outstretched arms to meet her husband. Dare and Luis were with him. They were black with the smoke of battle. Their clothing was torn and bloodstained; the awful light of the fierce struggle was still upon their faces. But they walked like heroes.

The men were hungry; they had eaten nothing all day. How delicious was their meal! How happy it made the Señora, and Antonia, and Isabel, to see them empty dish after dish; to see their unaffected enjoyment of the warm room and bright fire. There was only one drawback to the joy of the reunion—the absence of Jack.

"His disappointment will be greater than ours," said Jack's father. "To be present at the freeing of his native city, and to bring his first laurels to his mother, was the brightest dream Jack had. But Jack is a fine rider, and is not a very fine marksman; so it was decided to send him with Houston to the Convention. We expected him back before the attack on the city began. Indeed, we were waiting for orders from the Convention to undertake it."

"Then you fought without orders, father?"

"Well, yes, Antonia—in a way. Delays in war are as dangerous as in love. We were surrounded by dragoons, who scoured the country in every direction to prevent our foraging. San Antonio HAD to be taken. Soon done was well done. On the third of December Colonel Milam stepped in front of the ranks, and asked if two hundred of the men would go with him and storm the city. The whole eleven hundred stepped forward, and gave him their hands and their word. From them two hundred of the finest marksmen were selected."

"I have to say that was a great scene, mi Roberto."

"The greater for its calmness, I think. There was no shouting, no hurrahing, no obvious enthusiasm. It was the simple assertion of serious men determined to carry out their object."

"And you stormed San Antonio with two hundred men, Father?"

"But every man was a picked man. A Mexican could not show his head above the ramparts and live. We had no powder and ball to waste; I doubt if a single ball missed its aim."

"A Mexican is like a Highland Scot in one respect," said Dare. "He fights best with steel. They are good cavalry soldiers."

"There are no finer cavalry in the world than the horsemen from Santa Fe, Dare. But with powder and ball Mexicans trust entirely to luck; and luck is nowhere against Kentucky sharpshooters. Their balls very seldom reached us, though we were close to the ramparts. We gathered them up by thousands and sent them back with our double-Dupont powder. THEN they did damage enough. In fact, we have taken the Alamo with Mexican balls."

"Under what flag did you fight, Roberto?"

"Under the Mexican republican flag of 1824, though indeed, Maria, I do not think we had one in the camp. We were destitute of all the trappings of war—we had no uniforms, no music, no flags, no positive military discipline. But we had one heart and mind, and one object in view. This four days' fight has shown what men can do, who are moved by a single, grand idea."

The Señora lay upon a sofa; the doctor sat by her side. Gradually their conversation became more low and confidential. They talked of their sons and their probable whereabouts; of all that the Señora and her daughters had suffered from the disaffection of the servants; of the attitude taken by Fray Ignatius. The doctor noticed, without much surprise, that his wife's political sympathies were still in a state of transition and uncertainty. She could not avoid prophesying the speedy and frightful vengeance of Mexico. She treated the success at San Antonio as one of the accidents of war. She looked forward to an early renewal of hostilities.

"My countrymen are known to me, Roberto," she said, with a touch that was almost a hope of vengeance. "They have an insurmountable honor; they will revenge this insult to it in some terrible way. If the gracious Maria holds not the hands of Santa Anna, he will utterly destroy the Americans! He will be like a tiger that has become mad."

"I am not so much afraid of Santa Anna as of Fray Ignatius. Promise me, Maria, that you will not suffer yourself or our children to be decoyed by him into a convent. I should never see you again."

The discussion on this subject was long and eager. Antonia, talking with Dare a little apart, could not help hearing it and feeling great interest in her father's entreaties, even though she was discussing with Dare the plans for their future. For Dare had much to tell his betrothed. During the siege, the doctor had discovered that his intended son-in-law was a fine surgeon. Dare had, with great delicacy, been quite reticent on this subject, until circumstances made his assistance a matter of life and death. The doctor understood and appreciated the young man's silence.

"He thinks I might have a touch of professional jealousy—that I might suspect him of wanting a partnership as well as a wife." Robert Worth confided to his wife. "He wants to take his full share of the dangers of war, without getting behind the shield of his profession." These feelings the doctor understood, and he passed from Fray Ignatius to this pleasanter topic, gladly.

He told the Señora what a noble son they were going to have. He said, "When the war is over, Maria, my dear, he shall marry Antonia."

"And what do you say, Roberto, if I should give them the fine house on the Plaza that my brother Perfecto left me?"

"If you do that you will be the best mother in the world, Maria. I then will take Dare into partnership. He is good and clever, and I am a little weary of work. I shall enjoy coming home earlier to you. We will go riding and walking, and our courting days will begin again."

"Maria Santissima! How delightful that will be, Roberto! And as for our Isabel, shall we not make her happy also? Luis should have done as his own family have done. For a young man to go against his mother and his uncles, that is very wicked! But, if we forgive that fault, well, then, Luis is as good as good bread."

"I think so. He began the study of the law. He must finish it. He must learn the American laws also. I am not a poor man, Maria. I will give Isabel a fortune worthy of a Yturbide or a Flores—a fortune that will make her very welcome to the Alvedas."

The Señora clasped her husband's hand with a smile. They were sweetening their own happiness with making the happiness of their children. They looked first at Antonia. She sat with Dare, earnestly talking to him in a low voice. Isabel sat in a large chair, and Luis leaned on the back of it.

"My happiness is so great, Roberto, I am even tired of being happy. Call Rachela. I must go to sleep. Tonight I cannot even say an ave."

"God hears the unspoken prayer in your heart, Maria. Tonight let me help you upstairs. My arm is stronger than Rachela's."

She rose with a little affectation of greater weakness and lassitude than she really felt. But she wished to be weak, so that her Roberto might be strong—to be quite dependent on his care and tenderness. She let her daughters embrace her, and then offered her hand to Dare and Luis with so much grace and kindness that both young men were enchanted.

"It is to be seen that they are gentlemen," she said, as she went slowly upstairs on her husband's arm. "So handsome, too."

"And brave."

"They will make fine husbands," the Señora smiled, "like mine."

chapter 10

Antonia's Bible

The exalted state of mind which the victorious men had brought home with them did not vanish with sleep. The same heroic atmosphere was in the house in the morning. Antonia's face had a brightness upon it that never yet was the result of mere flesh and blood. When she came into the usual sitting-room, Dare was already there; indeed, he had risen purposely for this hour. Their smiles and glances met each other with an instantaneous understanding. Antonia went about busily ordering the breakfast and giving to the table a festal air, while Dare watched with admiration. The Señora did not come down; but Isabel and Luis and the doctor joined the breakfast party. Luis had evidently been to see Lopez Navarro before he did so, for he wore a new suit of dark blue velvet and silver, a sash of crimson silk, the neatest of patent leather shoes, and the most beautifully embroidered linen. Dare gave him a little smile and nod of approbation. He had not thought of fine clothing for himself—his own was still blackened with smoke; but then for the handsome, elegant Mexican youth it seemed precisely the right thing. Isabel, in her scarlet satin petticoat, and white embroideries and satin slippers, looked his proper mate.

The three women watched their heroes go back to the city. The doctor looked little older than his companions. He sat his horse superbly, and he lifted his hat to the proud Señora with a loving grace which neither of the young men could excel. In that far back year, when he had wooed her, he had not looked more manly and attractive. Never had the Señora loved her husband as she did at that hour.

In his capacity of physician he had done unnoticed deeds of far greater bravery—gone into a Comanche camp that was being devastated by smallpox—or galloped fifty miles, alone in the night, through woods haunted by savage men and beasts, to succor some little child struggling with croup, or a frontiersman pierced with an arrow. The Señora had always fretted and scolded a little when he thus exposed his life. But the storming of the Alamo! That was a bravery she could understand.

Rachela was in a state of rebellion. Nothing but the express orders of Fray Ignatius, to remain where she was, prevented her leaving the Worths, for the freedom so suddenly given to Isabel had filled her with indignation. She was longing to be in some house where she could give adequate expression to the diabolical temper she felt it right to indulge.

In the afternoon it was some relief to see the confessor coming up the garden. He had resumed his usual deliberate pace. His hands were folded upon his breast. He looked as the mournful Jeremiah may have looked, when he had the burden of a heavy prophecy to deliver.

The Señora sat down with a doggedly sullen air, which Antonia understood very well. It meant, "I am not to be

forced to take any way but my own, today." The wise
priest understood her mood as soon as he entered the
room. He put behind him the reproof he had been
meditating. He stimulated her curiosity; he asked her
sympathy. No man knew better than Fray Ignatius when
to assume sacerdotal authority and when to lay it aside.

And the Señora was never proof against the compliment of his personal friendship. The fight, as it affected
himself and his brotherhood and the convent, was full of
interest to her. She smiled at Brother Servando's childish
alarm; she was angry at an insult offered to the venerable
abbot; she condoled with the Sisters; and she wept at the
danger that the famous statue of the Virgin de Los
Reinedias had been exposed to. She was altogether as
sympathetic as he could desire, until her own affairs
were mentioned.

"And you also, my daughter? The sword has pierced
your heart too, I am sure! To know that your husband
and sons were fighting against your God and your country! Holy Mother! How great must have been your grief.
But, for your comfort, I tell you that the saints who have
suffered a fiery martyrdom stand at the feet of those
who, like you, endure the continual crucifixion of their
affections."

The Señora was silent, but not displeased and the
priest then ventured a little further:

"But there is an end to all trials, daughter, and I now
absolve you from the further struggle. Decide this day
for your God and your country. Make an offering to
Almighty God and the Holy Mother of your earthly love.
Give yourself and your daughters and all that you have to

the benign and merciful Church. Show these rebels and
heretics—these ungrateful recipients of Mexican
bounty—what a true Catholic is capable of. His Divine
Majesty and the Holy Mary demand this supreme sacrifice from you."

"Father, I have my husband, and my sons; to them,
also, I owe some duties."

"The Church will absolve you from them."

"It would break my heart."

"Listen then: If it is your right hand, or your right
eye—that is, if it is your husband, or your child—you are
commanded to give them up, or—it is God's word—there
is only hell fire."

"Mother of Sorrows, pity me! What shall I do?"

She looked with the terror of a child into the dark,
cruel face of the priest. It was as immovably stern as if
carved out of stone. Then her eyes sought those of
Antonia, who sat at a distant window with her embroidery in her hand. She let it fall when her mother's
pitiful, uncertain glance asked from her strength and
counsel. She rose and went to her. Never had the tall,
fair girl looked so noble. A sorrowful majesty, that had
something in it of pity and something of anger, gave to
her countenance, her movements, and even her speech, a
kind of authority.

"Dear mother, do as the beloved and kindhearted
Ruth did. Like you, she married one not of her race and
not of her religion. Even when God had taken him from
her, she chose to remain with his people—to leave her
own people and abide with his mother. For this act God
blessed her, and all nations in all ages have honored her."

"Ruth! What has Ruth to do with the question?" Fray Ignatius flared. "Presumptuous one! Ruth was a heathen woman—a Moabite—a race ten times accursed."

"Pardon, father. Ruth was the ancestress of our blessed Saviour and of the Virgin Mary."

"Believe not the wicked one, Señora. She is blinded with false knowledge. She is a heretic. I have long suspected it. She has not been to confession for nine months."

"You wrong me, father. Every day, twice a day, I confess my sins humbly."

"Chito![33] You are in outrageous sin. But, then, what else? I hear, indeed, that you read wicked books—even upon your knees you read them."

"I read my Bible, father."

"Bring it to me. How could a child like you read the Bible? It is a book for bishops and archbishops, and the Immaculate Father[34] himself. What an arrogance! What an insolence of self-conceit must possess so young a heart!"

The girl stood with burning cheeks gazing at the proud, passionate man, but she did not obey his order.

"Señora, my daughter! See you with your own eyes the fruit of your sin. Will you dare to become a partner in such wickedness?"

"Antonia! Go at once and bring here this wicked book. Oh, how can you make so miserable a mother who loves you so much?"

---

[33]Chito! [chē′tō]—Silence!
[34]Immaculate Father—the pope

In a few moments Antonia returned with the objectionable book. "My dear grandmother gave it to me," she said. "Look, mi madre, here is my name in her writing. Is it conceivable that she would give to your Antonia a book that she ought not to read?"

The Señora took it in her hands and turned the leaves very much as a child might turn those of a book in an unknown tongue, in which there were no illustrations nor anything that looked the least interesting. It was a pretty volume of moderate size, bound in purple morocco and fastened with gilt clasps.

"I see the word GOD in it very often, Fray Ignatius. Perhaps, indeed, it is not bad."

"It is a heretic Bible, I am sure. Could anything be more sinful, more disrespectful to God, more dangerous for a young girl?" And as he said the words he took it from the Señora's listless hands, glanced at the obnoxious title-page, and then, stepping hastily to the hearth, flung the book upon the burning logs.

With a cry of horror, pain, and amazement all blended, Antonia sprang towards the fire, but Fray Ignatius stood with outstretched arms before it.

"Stand back!" he cried. "To save your soul from eternal fires, I burn the book that has misled you!"

"Oh, my Bible! My Bible! Oh, mother!" Crying out in her fear and anger, the girl fled down the stairs and called the peasant Ortiz.

"Do you know where to find the Señor Doctor? If you do, Ortiz, take the swiftest horse and bring him here."

The man looked with anger into the girl's troubled face. For a moment he was something unlike himself. "I can find him; I will bring him in fifteen minutes. It is here he should be."

Antonia sat down at the window to watch for the result of her message. Fortunately, Rachela had been so interested in the proceedings, and so determined to know all about them, that she seized the opportunity of the outcry to fly to "her poor Señora," and thus was ignorant of this most unusual step taken by Antonia.

Indeed, no one was aware of it but herself and Ortiz, and the servants in the kitchen looked with a curious interest at the doctor riding into the stable yard as if life depended upon his speed. Perhaps it did. All of them stopped their work to speculate upon the circumstance.

They saw him fling himself from the saddle; they saw Antonia run to meet him; they heard her voice full of distress. Her tearful complaint was answered by a stamp of the doctor's iron-heeled boot on the stone floor of the hall and a fierce exclamation that rang through the whole house.

They heard the doctor mount the stairs, and then they were left to their imaginations. As for Antonia, she was almost terrified at the storm she had raised. Never had she seen anger so terrible. Yet, though he had not said a word directly to her, she was aware of his full sympathy. He grasped her hand, and entered the Señora's room with her. His first order was to Rachela—

"Leave the house in five minutes; no, in three minutes. I will tell Ortiz to send your clothes after you. Go!"

"My Señora! Fray I—"

"Go!" he thundered. "Out of my house! Fly! I will not endure you another moment."

The impetus of his words was like a great wind. They drove the woman before him, and he shut the door behind her with a terrifying and amazing rage. Then he turned to the priest—

"Fray Ignatius, you have abused my hospitality and my patience. You shall do so no longer. For twenty-six years I have suffered your interference—"

"The Señor is a prudent man. The wise bear what they cannot resist." With a gentle smile and lifted eyebrows Fray Ignatius crossed himself.

"I have respected your faith and your opinions, though they were false and cruel, because you believed honestly in them. But you shall not again interfere with my wife, or my children, or my servants, or my house."

"The Señor Doctor is not prince or pope. 'Shall,' and 'shall not,' no one but my own ecclesiastical superiors can say to me."

"I say, you shall not again terrify my wife and insult my daughter or disorganize my whole household! And, as the God of my mother hears me, you shall not again burn up His Holy Word under my roof. Never, while I dwell beneath it, shall you enter my gates, or cross my threshold, or address yourself to any that bear my name, or eat my bread." With the words, he walked to the door and held it open. It was impossible to mistake the unspoken order, and there was something in the concentrated yet controlled passion of Robert Worth which even the haughty priest did not care to irritate beyond its bounds.

He gathered his robe together and with lifted eyes muttered an ejaculatory prayer. Then he said in slow, cold, precise tones:

"For the present, I go. Very good. I shall come back again. The saints will take care of that. Señora, I give you my blessing. Señor, you may yet find the curse of a poor priest an inconvenience."

He crossed himself at the door and cast a last look at the Señora, who had thrown herself upon her knees and was crying out to Mary and the saints in a passion of excuses and reproaches. She was deaf to all her husband said. She would not suffer Antonia to approach her. She felt that now was the hour of her supreme trial. She had tolerated the rebellion of her husband, and her sons, and her daughter, and now she was justly punished. They had driven away her confessor and the maid who had been her counsellor and her reliance from her girlhood.

Her grief and terror were genuine and therefore pitiful, and, in spite of his annoyance, the doctor recognized the fact. In a moment, as soon as they were alone, he put aside his anger. He knelt beside her, he soothed her with tender words, he pleaded the justice of his indignation. And ere long she began to listen to him.

"My dear Maria, when the Americans have won Texas, they—"

"Saints in heaven, Roberto! That day comes not. One victory! Bah! That is an accident. The Mexicans are a very brave people—the bravest in the world. Did they not drive the Spaniards out of their country, and it is not to be contradicted that the Spaniards have conquered all other nations. That I saw in a book. The insult the Americans have given to Mexico will be revenged. Her honor has been compromised before the world. Very well, it will be made bright again; yes, Fray Ignatius says with blood and fire it will be made bright."

"And in the mean time, Maria, we have taken from them the city they love best of all. An hour ago I saw, General Cos, with 1,100 Mexican soldiers, pass before a little band of less than two hundred Americans and lay down their arms. These defenders of the Alamo had all been blessed by the priests. Their banners had been anointed with holy oil and holy water. They had all received absolution every day before the fight began; they had been promised a free passage through purgatory and a triumphant entry into heaven."

"Well, I will tell you something; Fray Ignatius showed it to me—it was a paper printed. The rebels and their wives and children are to be sent from this earth—you may know where they will all go, Roberto—Congress says so. The States will give their treasures. The archbishops will give the episcopal treasures. The convents will give their gems and gold ornaments. Ten thousand men have left for San Antonio, and ten thousand more are to follow, the whole under our great President Santa Anna. Oh, yes! The rebels in Washington are to be punished also. It is well known that they sent soldiers to Nacogdoches. Mexicans are not blind moles, and they have their intelligence, you know. All the States who have helped these outrageous ingrates are to be devastated, and you will see that your famous Washington will be turned into a heap of rubbish. I have seen these words in print, Roberto. I assure you, that it is not just a little breath—what one or another says—it is the printed order of the Mexican government. That is something these Americans will have to pay attention to."

The doctor sighed and answered the sorrowful, credulous woman with a kiss. What was the use of reasoning with simplicity so ignorant and so confident? He turned the conversation to a subject that always roused her best and kindest feelings—her son Jack.

"I have just seen young Dewees, Maria. He and Jack left San Felipe together. Dewees brought instructions to General Burleson, and Jack carried others to Fanning at Goliad."

She took her husband's hand. "That indeed! Oh, Roberto! If I could only see my Jack once more! I have had a constant accusation to bear about him. Till I kiss my boy again, the world will be all dark before my face. If Our Lady will grant me this miraculous favor, I will always afterwards be exceedingly religious. I will give all my desires to the other world."

"Dearest Maria, God did not put us in this world to be always desiring another. There is no need, mi queridita, to give up this life as a bad affair. We shall be happy again, soon."

"As you say. If I could only see Jack! For that, I would promise God Almighty and you, Roberto, to be happy. I would forgive the rebels and the heretics—for they are well acquainted with hell road, and will guide each other there without my wish."

"I am sure if Jack has one day he will come to you. And when he hears of the surrender of General Cos—"

"Well now, it was God's will that General Cos should surrender. What more can be said? It is sufficient."

"Let me call Antonia. She is miserable at your displeasure—it is not Antonia's fault."

"Pardon me, Roberto. I have seen Antonia. She is not agreeable and obedient to Fray Ignatius."

"She has been very wickedly used by him; I fear he intends to do her evil."

"It is not convenient to discuss the subject now. I will see Isabel; she is a good child—my only comfort. Paciencia! there is Luis Alveda singing. Isabel will now be deaf to all else," and she rose with a sigh and walked towards the casement looking into the garden.

Luis was coming up the oleander walk. The pretty trees were thinner now, with only a pink blossom here and there. But the bright winter sun shone through them and fell upon Luis and Isabel. For she had seen him coming and had gone to meet him. She seemed such a proper mate for the handsome youth at her side that a word of dissent was not possible. The doctor said only, "She is so like you, Maria. I remember when you were still more lovely, and when from your balcony you made me with a smile the happiest man in the world."

Such words were never lost ones; for the Señora had a true and great love for her husband. She gave him again a smile, she put her hand in his, and then there were no further conciliations required. They stood in the

sunshine of their own hearts and listened a moment to
the gay youth, singing, how at—

> The strong old Alamo
> Two hundred men, with rifles true,
> Shot down a thousand of the foe,
> And broke the triple ramparts through;
> And dropped the flag as black as night,
> For Freedom's green and red and white.[35]

chapter **11**

A Happy Truce

Cities have not only a certain physiognomy;[36] they
have also a decided mental and moral character
and a definite political tendency. There are good and
bad cities, artistic and commercial cities, scholarly and
manufacturing cities, aristocratic and radical cities. San
Antonio, in its political and social character, was a
thoroughly radical city. Its population, composed in a
large measure of adventurous units from various nation-
alities, had that fluid rather than fixed character, which
is susceptible to new ideas. For they were generally men

---

[35]The flag of the Mexican Republic of 1824 was green, red, and white in color.

[36]physiognomy—physical features revealing character

who had found the restraints of the centuries behind
them to be intolerable—men to whom freedom was
the grand ideal of life.

It may be easily understood that this element in
the population of San Antonio was a powerful one. A
little of such leaven could stir into activity a people
who, beneath the crust of their formal piety, had still
something left of that pride and adventurous spirit
which distinguished the Spain of Ferdinand and
Isabel.

In fact, no city on the American continent has such
a bloody record as San Antonio. From its settlement
by the warlike monks of 1692, to its final capture by
the Americans in 1836, it was well named "the city of
the sword." The Comanche and the white man fought
around its walls their forty years' battle for supremacy.
From 1810 to 1821 its streets were constantly bloody
with the fight between the royalists and republicans,
and the city and the citadel passed from one party to
the other continually. When it came to the question of
freedom and American domination, San Antonio was,
as it had ever been, the great Texan battlefield.

In the main there was a favorable feeling regarding
its occupation by the Americans. The most lawless of
them were law-abiding in comparison with any kind of
victorious Mexicans. Americans respected private
property, they honored women, they observed the
sanctity of every man's home. "And, as for being
heretics, that was an affair for the saints and the
priests; the comfortable benefits of the Holy Catholic
Church had not been vouchsafed to all nations."

Political changes are favorable to religious tolerance, and the priests themselves had been sensible of a great decrease in their influence during the pending struggle. Prominent Mexicans had given aid and comfort to the Americans in spite of their spiritual orders, and there were many men who, like Lopez Navarro, did not dare to go to confession, because they would have been compelled to acknowledge themselves rebels.

When the doctor and Dare and Luis reached the Plaza the morning after the surrender, they found the city already astir. Thousands of women were in the churches saying masses for the dead. The men stood at their store doors or sat smoking on their balconies, chatting with the passers-by or watching the movements of the victorious army and the evacuation of the conquered one.

Nearly all of the brave two hundred occupied the Plaza. They were still greatly excited by the miraculous ecstasy of victory. All things seemed possible to them. The confidence of their carriage and the authority in their faces gave dignity even to their deerskin clothing.

Lopez Navarro touched the doctor and directed his attention to them. "Does the world, Señor, contain the stuff to make their counterparts?"

"They are Americans, Navarro. And though there are a variety of Americans, they have only one opinion about submitting to tyrants—they won't do it!"

This was the conversation interrupted by Ortiz and the message he brought, and the doctor was thoroughly sobered by the events following. He was not inclined to believe, as the majority of the troops did, that Mexico was conquered. He expected that the Señora's prediction would be verified. The personal enmity which the priesthood felt to him induced a depressing sense of personal disaster.

Nothing in the house or the city seemed inclined to settle. It took a few days to draw up the articles of capitulation and clear the town of General Cos and the Mexican troops. Worth had no faith in their agreement to "retire from Texas, and never again carry arms against the Americans." He knew that they did not consider it any sin to make "a mental reservation" against a heretic. He was quite sure that if Cos met reinforcements, he would be back.

Amid these public cares and considerations, the doctor had serious private ones. The Señora was still under the control of Fray Ignatius. It required all the influence of his own personal presence and affection to break the spiritual captivity in which he held her. He knew that the priest had long been his enemy.

He saw that Antonia, in particular, was hated by him. She was in the shadow of a terror worse than death—that of a long, hopeless captivity. A dungeon and a convent might become to them a living grave, in which cruelty and despair would slowly gnaw life away.

Yet, for a day or two he resolved not to speak of his terror. The Señora was so happy in his presence, and she had such kind confidences to give him about her plans for her children's future, that he could not bear to alarm her. And the children also were so full of youth's enthusiasms and love's sweet dreams. Till the last moment why should he awaken them?

The Señora came to the parlor far more frequently, and in her own apartments her children visited her with but slight ceremony. They discussed all together their future plans. They talked over a wonderful journey which they were to take in company to New Orleans, and Washington, and New York, and perhaps even to London and Paris—"who could tell, if the Señora would be so good as to enjoy herself?" They ate more together. They got into the habit of congregating about the same hearth-stone. It was the Señora's first real experience of domestic life.

In about six days the Mexican forces left the city. The terms of surrender granted General Cos struck the Mexicans with a kind of wonder. They had fought with the express declaration that they would take no American prisoner. Yet the Americans not only permitted Cos and his troops to leave under parole of honor, but gave them their arms and sufficient ammunition to protect themselves from the Indians on their journey home. They allowed them also all their private property. They furnished them with the provisions necessary to reach the Rio Grande. They took charge of their sick and wounded. They set all the Mexican prisoners at liberty— in short, so great was their generosity and courtesy that the Mexicans were unable to comprehend their motives.

Even Lopez was troubled at it. "I assure you," he said to Dr. Worth, "they will despise such civility; they will not believe in its sincerity. At this very blessed hour, they are accusing the Americans of being afraid to press their advantage. Simply, you will have the fight to make over again. I say this, because I know Santa Anna."

"Santa Anna is but a man, Lopez."

"Me perdonas![37] He is however a man who knows a trick more than the devil. One must be careful of a bull in front, of a mule behind, and of a monk and Santa Anna on all sides." At the word monk, Lopez glanced significantly at a passing priest, and Doctor Worth saw that it was Fray Ignatius.

"He sprinkled the Mexican troops with holy water and blessed them as they left the city this morning. He has the ear of General Cos. He is not a man to offend, I assure you, Doctor."

The doctor walked thoughtfully away. San Antonio was full of his friends, yet never had he felt himself and his family to be in so much danger. The words of Lopez had struck a responding chord in his own consciousness. The careless bravery, the splendid generosity of his countrymen was at least premature. He went through the city with observing eyes, and he saw much to trouble him.

The gates of Alamo were open. Crockett lounged upon his rifle in the Plaza. A little crowd was around him, and the big Tennesseean hunter was talking to them. Shouts of laughter and bravas of enthusiasm answered the homely wit and stirring speech that had over and over "made room for Colonel Crockett," both in the Tennessee Legislature and the United States Congress. The young fellows around found in him their ideal of a leader.

The elegant James Bowie was sitting on the verandah of the Veramendi House. His fair, handsome face, clear

---

[37]Me perdonas! [mä pĕr·dōn′*a*s]—Forgive me

blue eyes, and mild manners gave no indication of the gigantic physical strength and tremendous coolness and courage of the man. Burleson and Travis were talking under the shade of a China tree, and there were little groups of American soldiers on every street. This was what he saw, and yet a terrible sense of insecurity oppressed him.

The city, moreover, was not settling to its usual business, though there were many preparations for public and private entertainments. After passing Colonel Bowie, he met David Burnett. The shrewd statesman from New Jersey had a shadow upon his face. He stopped Doctor Worth and spoke frankly to him. "We are in greater danger now than when we were under fire," he said. "Santa Anna will come on us like a lion from the swellings of Jordan. I wish Houston knew our position as it really is. We must either have more men to defend this city or we must blow up the Alamo and be ready to leave it at a moment's notice."

"Why were such favorable terms given to General Cos and his troops? I cannot understand it."

"I will tell you an amazing fact. When Cos ran up that white flag on the Alamo, we had not a single round of ammunition left. Complaisance was necessary until Cos made over to us the Mexican arms, ammunition, property, and money."

Worth turned and looked at the fort. A great red flag on which was the word T-E-X-A-S floated from its battlements, and there were two men standing on its roof, with their faces westward.

"They are the lookouts," said Burnett, "and we have scouts through the surrounding country; but Santa Anna will come, when he comes, with tens of thousands."

"And there is a line where even the coolest courage and the most brilliant bravery succumbs to mere numbers—Eh!"

"That is what I mean, Doctor."

"Where is Houston?"

"On the Brazos, at the small town of Washington. The council have established headquarters there."

Dangers postponed make even the most timorous indifferent to them. When General Cos did not return, and nothing was heard of Santa Anna, everyone began to take up their ordinary life again. The temper of the Americans also encouraged this disposition. They were discovered neither to be bloodthirsty nor cannibals. It was even seen that they enjoyed the fandango[38] and the monte[39] tables, and that a proposition for a bullfight at Christmas was not opposed by them.

On Christmas Eve the old city was very gay. The churches were decorated, and splendidly dressed men and women passed in and out with smiles and congratulations. From the huertas[40] around, great numbers of families had come to receive absolution and keep the Nativity. Their rich clothing and air of idleness gave a holiday feeling to the streets noisy with the buzzing of the guitar, the metallic throb of the cithara,[41] the murmurs of

---

[38]fandango [făn·dăng′ô]—a lively Spanish dance

[39]monte [mŏn′tē]—a card game

[40]huertas [hwĕr′täs]—farms

[41]cithara [sĭth′ə·rə]—a stringed instrument resembling a lyre

voices, and the cries of the hawkers. Priests, Mexicans, Indians, and Americans touched each other on the narrow thoroughfares, but that indescribable feeling of good will which comes with Christmas pervaded the atmosphere, and gave, even in the midst of war and danger, a sense of anticipated pleasure.

At the Worth residence there was a household feast. The Señora and her daughters were in full dress. They were waiting for the dear ones who had promised to join them at the Angelus. One by one the houses around were illuminated. Parties of simple musicians began to pass each other continually—they were going to serenade the blessed Mary all night long. As Antonia closed the balcony window, half a dozen of these young boys passed the garden hedge, singing to the clacking of their castanets—

"This is the eve of Christmas,
No sleep from night to morn,
The Virgin is in travail,
At twelve will the Child be born."

Luis appeared at the same moment. He caught up the wild melody and came up the garden path singing it. Dare and the doctor followed him. It struck Antonia that they were talking of a change, or of something important. But there was no time for observation. Isabel, radiant in crimson satin, with a white mantilla over her head, darted forward to meet Luis. Dare and the doctor took Antonia's hands, and there was something in the silent clasp of each which made her heart tremble.

But she was not one to enquire after misfortune. She could wait and let the evil news find her, and by so doing she won many a bright hour from the advancing shadows.

The Señora was in unusual spirits. She had obtained a
new confessor. "A man of the most seraphic mind, and,
moreover, so fortunate as to be connected with the house
of Flores." He had been gentle to her in the matter of
penances and had not set her religious obligations above
her capacities. Consequently, the Señora had laid aside
her penitential garments. She was in full Castilian costume and looked very handsome. But Antonia, who had
been in New York during those years when she would
otherwise have been learning how to wear a mantilla and
use a fan, knew that she would look unnatural in them,
and she adhered to the American fashions of her day.
Dressed in a plain frock of dark satin, she exhibited a
simple, noble beauty.

The meal was a very merry one, and after it Lopez
Navarro joined the party and they had music and dancing, finally gathering around the fire to hear the singing
of Luis. He knew a great many of the serenades, and as
he sang of the Virgin and the Babe, a more solemn joy
came to each heart.

"How sweet and wild are these serenades, Luis!" said
Antonia. "I wonder who wrote them?"

"They were never written, my sister. Out of the
hearts of lonely shepherds they came, or of women
spinning in their quiet houses, and yes, even of soldiers
in the strong places keeping their watch."

"That is the truth, Luis," answered Isabel. "And every
Christmas, when I was in the convent, the Sisters made a
serenade to the Virgin, or a seguidilla[42] to our blessed

---

[42]seguidilla [sā′gê·dē′yə]—a Spanish verse set to music

Lord. Very still are the Sisters, but when it comes to singing, I can assure you the angels might listen!"

"There is a seguidilla I hear everywhere," said the doctor, "and I never hear it without feeling the better for listening. It begins—'So noble a Lord.'"

"That, indeed!" cried Luis. "Who knows it not? It is the seguidilla to our blessed Lord, written by the daughter of Lope de Vega—the holy Marcela Carpio. You know it, Señora?"

"As I know my credo, Luis."

"And you, Isabel?"

"Since I was a little one, as high as my father's knee. Rachela taught it to me."

"And you, Lopez."

"That is sure, Luis."

"And I, too!" said Antonia, smiling. "Here is your mandolin. Strike the chords, and we will all sing with you. My father will remember also." And the doctor smiled an assent, as the young man resigned Isabel's hand with a kiss, and swept the strings in that sweetness and power which flows invisibly, but none the less surely, from the heart to the instrument.

"It is to my blessed Lord and Redeemer, I sing," he said, bowing his head. Then he stood up and struck the key note, and everyone joined their voices with his in the wonderful little hymn:

> So noble a Lord
>   None serves in vain;
> For the pay of my love
>   Is my love's sweet pain.

In the place of caresses
  Thou givest me woes;
I kiss Thy hands,
  When I feel their blows.

For in Thy chastening,
  Is joy and peace;
O Master and Lord!
  Let thy blows not cease.

I die with longing
  Thy face to see
And sweet is the anguish
  Of death to me.

For, because Thou lovest me,
  Lover of mine!
Death can but make me
  Utterly Thine!

The doctor was the first to speak after the sweet triumph of the notes had died away. "Many a soul I have seen pass whispering those verses," he said, "men and women, and little children."

"The good Marcela in heaven has that for her joy," answered Luis.

Lopez rose while the holy influence still lingered. He kissed the hands of everyone, and held the doctor's in his own until they reached the threshold. A more than usual farewell took place there, though there were only a few whispered words.

"Farewell, Lopez! I can trust you?"

"Unto death."

"If we never meet again?"

"Still it will be *farewell*. Thou art in God's care."

Very slowly the doctor sauntered back to the parlor, like a man who has a heavy duty to do and hardly knows how to begin it. "But I will tell Maria first," he whispered, and then he opened the door and saw the Señora bidding her children good-night.

"What a happy time we have had!" she was saying. "I shall never forget it. Indeed, my dears, you see how satisfactory it is to be religious. When we talk of the saints and angels, they come round us to listen to what we say; accordingly, we are full of peace and pleasure. I know that because I heard Fray—I heard a very good man say so."

She smiled happily at her husband as she took his arm, and twice, as they went slowly upstairs together, she lifted her face for his kiss. Her gentleness and affection made it hard for him to speak; but there were words to be said that could be no longer delayed. As he closed the door, he took her hands in his and looked into her face with eyes that told her all.

"You are going away, Roberto," she whispered.

"Yes, my love! Tonight—this very hour I must go! Luis and Dare also. Do not weep. I entreat you! My heart is heavy, and your tears I cannot bear."

Then she answered, with a noble composure: "I will give you smiles and kisses, my good Roberto, so true and kind! I will try to be worthy of you. Nay, but you must not weep—!"

It was true. Quite unconsciously the troubled husband and father was weeping. "I fear to leave you,

dear Maria. All is so uncertain. I can only ask you two
favors; if you will grant them, you will do all that can be
done to send me away with hope. Will you promise me to
have nothing to do whatever with Fray Ignatius, and to
resist every attempt he may make to induce you to go into
a religious house of any kind?"

"I promise you, Roberto. By my mother's cross, I
promise you!"

"Again, dear Maria, if you should be in any danger,
promise me that you will do as Antonia and Lopez
Navarro think is wisest and best."

"Go with God, my husband. Go with God, in a good
hour. All you wish, I will do."

He held her to his heart and kissed her, and she whispered amid her tender farewells, "Will you see Juan? If
you do, tell him I repent. I send him a thousand blessings!
Kiss him for me, Roberto! Tell him how much I love him,
Roberto! How I sorrow because I was cross to him!"

At length Isabel came in to weep in her mother's arms.
"Luis is going away," she cried. The father felt a momen-
tary pang of jealousy. "I am going also, queridita," he said
mournfully. Then she threw her arms around his neck
and bewailed her bad fortune.

While the Señora soothed her complaining, the doctor
left. One troubled glance he cast backward from the door
ere he closed it behind him, and then his countenance
suddenly changed. Stern and strong it grew, with a glow
of anger in the steel-blue eyes that gave an entirely new
character to it.

He called Antonia into his study, and talked with her of
the crisis which was approaching and of the conduct of

their affairs in it. He showed her the places in which his gold coin was hidden. He told her on whom to rely in any emergency.

"We have sure information that General Urrea, with the vanguard of a large Mexican army, will be here next month. Santa Anna will follow him quickly. You see that the city must either be defended or our men must retreat. I am going to Houston with this dilemma. Luis and Dare will join Fanning at Goliad. Now, my child, you have my place to fill. If Santa Anna takes possession of San Antonio, what will you do?"

"If we are not disturbed in any way, I will keep very quiet within my own home."

"If Fray Ignatius attempts to interfere with you— what then?"

"I will fly from him, and take Isabel and mi madre with me."

"That is your only safety. I shall hear if the Americans desert the city; then I will send your brother Thomas, if by any possibility it can be done, to guard you to the eastern settlements. But I may not be able to do this—there may be no time. Lopez Navarro will help you all he can, and you may always rely on Ortiz."

"My father, I cannot trust Ortiz. Every man is a master to a peasant. He would mean to do kindly, but his cowardice might make him false."

"Ortiz is no peasant. He is a Mexican officer of high rank, whom Santa Anna ordered to be shot. I saved his life. He wears the clothes of a peasant—that is necessary—but he has the honor and gratitude of a gentleman beneath them. If necessary, trust Ortiz fully.

One thing above all others remember: *Flight* before a convent."

"Flight! Yes, death before it! I promise you, Father. When we meet again, you shall say, 'Well done, Antonia.' "

It was now about midnight. They went back to the parlor. Luis and Dare sat by the dying fire. They were bent forward, talking in a low voice. They rose when the doctor spoke, and silently kissed Antonia.

"It is time, men," said the doctor. Antonia walked with them to the rear of the house where their horses were standing ready saddled. Silently the men mounted. In a moment they had passed the gate, and the beat of their horses' hoofs died away.

But all through the clear spaces of the sky the Christmas bells were ringing, and the serenaders were singing to each other,

"At twelve will the Child be born!"

chapter 12

Danger and Help

D r. Worth had set his daughter a task of no light magnitude. It was true that Rachela and Fray Ignatius could no longer disturb the household by their actual presence, but their power to cause unhappiness was not destroyed. Among the Mexican families loyal to Santa Anna, the dismission of the priest and the duenna had been a source of much indignant gossip, for Rachela was one of those women who cry out when they are hurt and compel others to share their trouble. The priest had not therefore found it necessary to explain WHY the Señora had called upon a new confessor. He could be silent and possess his dignity in uncomplaining patience, while Rachela paraded his wrongs as a kind of set-off to her own.

Such piety! Such virtues! And the outrageous conduct of the Señor Doctor! To be sure there was cause for anger at the Señorita Antonia. Oh, yes! She could crow her mind abroad! There were books—Oh, infamous books! Books not proper to be read, and the Señorita had them! Well then, if the father burned them, that was a good deed done. And he had almost been reviled for it—sent out of the house—yes, it was quite possible that he had been struck! Anything was possible from those

American heretics. As for her own treatment, after
twenty years service, it had been cruel, abominable, more
than that—iniquitous. But the day of atonement would
come. Justice was informing itself on the whole matter.

Such conversations continually diversified, extended,
and repeated on all hands quickly aroused a prejudice
against the doctor's family. Besides which, the Señora
Alveda resented bitterly the visits of her son Luis to
Isabel. None of the customs of a Mexican betrothal had
taken place, and Rachela did not spare her imagination
in describing the scandalous American familiarity that
had been permitted. That this familiarity had taken place
under the eyes of the doctor and the Señora only intensified the insult. She might have forgiven clandestine
meetings, but that the formalities due to the Church and
herself should have been neglected was indeed unpardon-
able.

It soon became evident to the Señora that she had
lost the good-will of her old friends and the respect that
had always been given to her social position. It was
difficult for her to believe this, and she only accepted the
humiliating fact after a variety of those small insults
which women reserve for their own sex.

She was fond of visiting; she valued the good opinion
of her caste. In the very chill of the gravest calamities she
worried her strength away over little grievances lying
outside the walls of her home and the real affections of
her life. And perhaps with perfect truth she asserted that
she had done nothing to deserve this social ostracism.
Others had made her miserable, but she could thank the
saints none could make her guilty.

The defeat of Cos had been taken by the loyal in-
habitants as a mere preliminary to the real fight. They
were very little disturbed by it. It was the overt act
which was necessary to convince Mexico that her
clemency to Americans was a mistake. The newspapers
heralded the coming of Santa Anna, the victorious
avenger, with passionate gasconading. It was a mere
question of a few days or weeks, and in the meantime
the people of San Antonio were "making a little profit
and pleasure to themselves out of the extravagant
reprobates." There was not a day in which they did not
anticipate their revenge in local military displays, in
dances and illuminations, in bull-fights, and in splendid
religious processions.

Antonia found it impossible to combat this influence. It was in the house as certain flavors are in
certain foods, or as heat is in fire. She saw it in the
faces of her servants, and felt it in their indifference to
their duty. Every hour she watched more anxiously for
some messenger from her father. And day after day, she
grew more restless under the continual trials that
encompassed her.

Toward the end of January, General Urrea entered
Texas at the head of the vanguard of the Mexican army.
His destination was La Bahia or Goliad, a strong for-
tress garrisoned by Americans under Colonel Fanning.
Santa Anna was to leave eight days after him. With an
army of 20,000 men he was coming to the relief of San
Antonio.

The news filled the city with the wildest rejoicing.
The little bells of the processions, the big bells of the

churches, the firing of cannon, and the hurrahs of the
multitudes made an uproar which reached the three
lonely women through the closed windows of their
rooms.

"If only Lopez Navarro would come! If he would
send us some little message!" cried the Señora.

At that moment the door opened, and Fray Ignatius
passed the threshold with lifted hands and a muttered
blessing. He approached the Señora, and she fell on her
knees and kissed the hand with which he crossed her.

"Holy father!" she cried, "the angels sent you to a
despairing woman."

"My daughter, I have guided you since your first
communion; how then could I forget you? Your husband
has deserted you—you, the helpless, tender lamb, whom
he swore to cherish. But the blessed fold of your church
stands open. Come, poor weary one, to its shelter."

"My father—"

"Listen to me! The Mexican troops are soon to arrive.
Vengeance without mercy is to be dealt out. You are the
wife of an American rebel; I cannot promise you your
life, or your honor, if you remain here. When soldiers are
drunk with blood, and women fall in their way, God have
mercy upon them! I would shield even your rebellious
daughter Antonia from such a fate. I open the doors of
the convent to you all. There you will find safety and
peace."

Isabel sat with white, parted lips and clasped hands,
listening. Antonia had not moved or spoken. But with
these last words the priest half-turned to her, and she
came swiftly to her mother's side.

"Remember your promise to my father! Oh, mi madre, do not leave Isabel and me alone!"

"You, too, dear ones! We will all go together, till these dreadful days are past."

"No, no! Isabel and I will not go. We will die rather."

"The Señorita talks like a foolish one. Listen again! When Santa Anna comes for judgment, it will be swift and terrible. This house and estate will be forfeited. The faithful Church may hope righteously to obtain it. The sisters have long needed a good home. The convent will then come to you. You will have no shelter but the Church. Come to her arms ere her entreaties are turned to commands."

"My husband told me—"

"Señora, you have no husband. He has forfeited every right to advise you. Consider that, daughter. And if you trust not my advice, there is yet living your honorable uncle, the Marquis de Gonzaga."

Antonia caught eagerly at this suggestion. It at least offered some delay in which the Señora might be strengthened to resist the coercion of Fray Ignatius.

"Mother, it is a good thought. My great-uncle will tell you what to do, and my father will not blame you for following his advice. Perhaps even he may offer his home. You are the child of his sister."

Fray Ignatius walked towards the fireplace and stood rubbing his long, thin hands before the blaze, while the Señora and her daughters discussed this proposal. The half-frantic mother was little inclined to make any further effort to resist the determined will of her old confessor, but the tears of Isabel won from her a promise to see her uncle.

"Then, my daughter, lose no time. I cannot promise you many days in which choice will be left you. Go this afternoon, and tomorrow I will call for your decision."

It was not a visit that the Señora liked to make. She had deeply offended her uncle by her marriage, and their intercourse had since been of the most ceremonious and infrequent kind. But surely, at this hour, when she was left without any one to advise her steps, he would remember the tie of blood between them.

He received her with more kindness than she had anticipated. His eyes glittered in their deep sockets when she related her extremity and the priest's proposal, and his small shrunken body quivered with excitement as he answered:

"Saints and angels! Fray Ignatius is right about Santa Anna. He will make caps for his soldiers out of the skins of these infidels. But as for going into the convent, I know not. A miserable marriage you made for yourself, Maria. Pardon, if I say so much! I let the word slip always. I was never one to bite my tongue. I am all old man—very well, come here, you and your daughters, till the days of blood are over. There is room in the house, and a few comforts in it also. I have some power with Santa Anna. He is a great man—a great man! In all his wars, good fortune flies before him."

He kissed her hand as he opened the door, and then went back to the fire, and bent, muttering, over it: "Giver of good! a true Yturbide—a gentle woman—she is like my sister Mercedes. These poor women who trust me, as I am a sinner before God, I am unhappy to deceive them."

Fray Ignatius might have divined his thoughts, for he entered at the moment, and said as he approached him:

"You have done right. The soul must be saved, if all is lost. This is not a time for the friends of the Church and of Mexico to waver. The Church is insulted every day by these foreign heretics—"

"But you are mistaken, father; the Church holds up her head, whatever happens. Even the vice-regal crown is not lost—the Church has cleft it into mitres."

Fray Ignatius smiled, but there was a curious and crafty look of inquiry on his face. "The city is turbulent, Marquis, and there is undoubtedly a great number of Mexicans opposed to Santa Anna."

"Do you not know Mexicans yet? They would be opposed to God Almighty, rather than confess they were well governed. Bah! the genius of Mexico is mutiny. They scarcely want a leader to move their madness. They rebel on any weak pretence. They bluster when they are courted; they crouch when they are oppressed. They are fools to all the world but themselves. I beg the Almighty to consider in my favor, that some over-hasty angel misplaced my lot. I should have been born in— New York."

The priest knew that he was talking for irritation, but he was too politic to favor the mood. He stood on the hearth with his hands folded behind him, and with a delightful suavity turned the conversation upon the country rather than the people. It was a glorious day in the dawn of spring. The tenderest greens, the softest

blues, the freshest scents, the clearest air, and the most
delightful sunshine were everywhere. The white old
town, with its picturesque crowds, its murmur of
voices and laughter, its echoes of fife and drum, its
loves and its hatreds, was at his feet, and far off stood
the hazy glory of the mountains. The old marquis was
insensibly led to contemplate the whole and, in so
doing, to put uppermost that pride of country which
was the base of every feeling susceptible to the priest's
influence.

"Such a pleasant city, Marquis! Spanish monks
founded it. Spanish and Mexican soldiers have defended it. Look at its fine churches and missions, its
lovely homes, and blooming gardens."

"It is also all our own, father. It was but yesterday I
said to one of those insolent Americans who was
condescending to admire it: 'Very good, Señor; and, if
you deign to believe me, it was not brought from New
York. Such as you see it, it was made by ourselves
here at San Antonio.' He laughed in my face. We were
mutually convinced of each other's stupidity."

"Ah, how they envy us the country! And you,
Marquis, who have traveled over the world, you can
imagine the reason?"

"Father, I will tell you the reason: it is the craving
in the heart to find again the lost Eden. The Almighty
made Texas with full hands. When He sets his heart
on a man, he is permitted to live there."

"Santa Maria! You speak the truth. Shall we then
give up the gift of His hand to heretics and infidels?"

"I cannot imagine it."

"Then every one must do the work he can do. Some are to slay the unbelievers; others are to preserve the children of the Church. Your niece and her two daughters will be lost to the faith unless you interfere for their salvation. Of you will their souls be required."

"By Saint Joseph, it is a duty not in agreement with my desire! I, who have carefully abstained from the charge of a wife and daughters of my own."

"It is but for a day or two, Marquis, until the matter is arranged. The convent is the best of all refuges for women so desolate."

The marquis did not answer. He lifted a book and began to read, and Fray Ignatius slipped quietly away.

In the mean time, the Señora had reached her home. She was pleased with the result of her visit. A little kindness easily imposed upon this childlike woman, and she trusted in anyone who was pleasant to her.

"You may believe me, Antonia," she said. "My uncle was in a temper most unusual. He kissed my hand. He offered me his protection. That is a great thing, I assure you. And your father cannot object to our removal there."

Antonia knew not what answer to make. Her heart misgave her. Why had Fray Ignatius made the proposal? She was sure it was part of an arrangement, and not a spontaneous suggestion of the moment. And she was equally sure that any preconcerted plan, having Fray Ignatius for its author, must be inimical to them.

Her mother's entry had not awakened Isabel, who lay asleep upon a sofa. The Señora was a little nettled at the circumstance. "She is a very child! A visit of such importance! And she is off to the land of dreams while I am fatiguing myself! I wish indeed that she had more consideration!" Antonia brought her chocolate, and, as she drank it, she chatted in an almost eager way about the persons she had seen.

"Going towards the Plaza, I met Judge Valdez. I stopped the carriage, and sent my affections to the Señora. Would you believe it? He answered me as if his mouth were full of snow. His disagreeable behavior was exactly copied by the Señora Silvestre and her daughter Esperanza. Doña Julia and Pilar de Calval did not even perceive me. Santa Maria! there are none so blind as those who won't see! Oh, indeed! I found the journey like the way of salvation—full of humiliations. I would have stopped at the store of the Jew Lavenburg and ordered many things, but he turned in when he saw me coming. Once, indeed, he would have put his hat on the pavement for me to tread upon. But he has heard that your father has made a rebel of himself, and what can be expected? He knows when Santa Anna has done with the rebels not one of them will have anything left for God to rain upon. And there was a great crowd and a great tumult. I think the whole city had a brain fever."

At this moment Isabel began to moan in her sleep as if her soul was in some intolerable terror or grief, and ere Antonia could reach her she sprang up with a shriek that rang through the house.

It was some minutes before the child could be soothed. She lay in her mother's arms, sobbing in speechless distress; but at length she was able to articulate her fright:

"Listen, mi madre, and may the Holy Lady make you believe me! I have had a dream. God be blessed that it is not yet true! I will tell you. It was about Fray Ignatius and our uncle the Marquis de Gonzaga. As my blessed Lord lives, I will not go to them! Si! I will cut my white throat first!" and she drew her small hand with a passionate gesture across it. She had stood up as she began to speak, and the action, added to her unmistakable terror, her stricken face, and air of determination, was very impressive.

"You have had a dream, my darling?"

"Yes, an awful dream, Antonia!"

"And you think we should not go to the house of the marquis?"

"Oh, Antonia! I have seen the way. It is black and cold, and full of fear and pain. No one shall make me take it. I have the stiletto of my grandmother Flores. I will ask the Holy One to pardon me, and then—in a moment—I would be among the people of the other world. That would be far better than Fray Ignatius and the house of Gonzaga."

The Señora was quite angry at this fresh complication. It was really incredible what she had to endure. And would Antonia please to tell her where else they were to go? They had not a friend left in San Antonio— they did not deserve to have one—and was it to be supposed that a lady, born noble, could follow the Americans in an ox-wagon? Antonia might think it preferable to the comfortable house of her relation, but blessed be the hand of God, which had opened the door of a respectable shelter to her.

"I will go in the ox-wagon," said Isabel, with a sullen determination, "but I will not go into my uncle's house. By the saint of my birth I swear it."

"Mother, listen to me," Antonia interceded. "When one door shuts, God opens another door. Our own home is yet undisturbed. Do you believe what Fray Ignatius says of the coming of Santa Anna? I do not. Until he arrives we are safe in our own home; and when the hour for going away comes, even a little bird can show us the way to take. And I am certain that my father is planning for our safety. If Santa Anna was in this city, and behaving with the brutality which is natural to him, I would not go away until my father sent the order. Do you think he forgets us? Be not afraid of such a thing. It cannot take place."

Toward dusk Señor Navarro called, and the Señora brought him into her private parlor and confided to him the strait they were in. He looked with sympathy into the troubled, tear-stained faces of these three helpless women, and listened with many expressive gestures to the proposal of the priest and the offer of the old marquis.

"Most excellent ladies," he answered, "it is a plot. I assure you that it is a plot. Certainly it was not without reason I was so unhappy about you this afternoon. Even while I was at the bull-fight, I think our angels were in a consultation about your affairs. Your name was in my ears above all other sounds."

"You say it is a plot, Señor. What do you mean?"

"I will tell you. Do you know that Fray Ignatius is the confessor of the marquis?"

"We had not thought of such a thing."

"It is the truth. For many years they have been close as the skin and the flesh. Without Fray Ignatius the marquis says neither yes or no. Also the will of the marquis has been lately made. I have seen a copy of it. Everything he has is left to the brotherhoods of the Church. Without doubt, Fray Ignatius was the lawyer who wrote it."

"Señor, I always believed that would happen. At my marriage my uncle made the determination. Indeed, we have never expected a peso. And today he was kind to me, and offered me his home. Oh, Holy Mother, how wretched I am! Can I not trust in the good words of those who are of my own family?"

"The tie of race will come before the tie of the family, and the tie of religion is strongest of all, Señora. Let me tell you what will take place. When you and your children are in the house of the marquis, he will go before the Alcalde.[43] He will declare that you have gone voluntarily to his care, and that he is your nearest and most natural guardian. Very well. But further, he will declare, on account of his great age, and the troubled state of the time, he is unable to protect you. He will then ask for the authority to place you in the religious care of the holy sisterhood of Saint Maria, and he will obtain all he wants."

"But what is to be gained by such treachery? He said today that I was like his sister Mercedes, and he spoke so gently to me."

---

[43]Alcalde [äl·käl′dĕ]—mayor

"He would not think such a proceeding really unkind. He would assure himself that it was good for your eternal salvation. As to the reason, that is to be looked for in the purse, where all reasons come from. This house, which the good doctor built, is the best in the city. It has even two full stories. It is very suitable for a religious house. It is not far from the Plaza, yet secluded in its beautiful garden. Fray Ignatius has long desired it. When he has removed you, possession will be taken, and Santa Anna will confirm the possession."

"God succor our poor souls! What shall we do then, Señor? The Mexican army has entered Texas; it will soon be here."

"Quien sabe? Between the Rio Grande and the San Antonio are many difficulties. Urrea has 5,000 men with him, horses and artillery. The horses must graze, the men must rest and eat. We shall have heavy rains. I am sure that it will be twenty days ere he reaches the settlements; and even then his destination is not San Antonio, it is Goliad. Santa Anna will be at least ten days after him. I suppose, then, that for a whole month you are quite safe in your own home. That is what I believe now. If I saw a reason to believe what is different, I would inform you. The good doctor, to whom I owe my life many times, has my promise. Lopez Navarro never broke his word to any man. The infamy would be a thing impossible."

"And in a month, mi madre, what great things may happen!" cried Isabel. "Thirty days of possibilities! Come, now, let us be a little happy, and listen to what the Señor has to tell us. I am sure this house has been as stupid as a convent!"

The Señora was swayed as easily as a child by the nearest or strongest influence. After all, it did seem the best to take Isabel's advice, and be a little happy while she could.

Lopez was delighted to humor this mood. He told them all the news of their own social set. In such vivid times something happened every day. There had been betrothals and marriages, quarrels and entertainments; and Lopez, as a fashionable young man of wealth and nobility, had taken his share in what had transpired.

Antonia felt unspeakably grateful to him. After the fretful terror and anxiety of the day—after the cruel visit of Fray Ignatius—it was indeed a comfort to hear the pleasant voice of Navarro in all kinds of cheerful modulations. By and by there was a slow rippling laugh from Isabel, and the Señora's face lost its air of dismal distraction.

At length Navarro had brought his narrative of small events down to the afternoon of that day. There had been a bullfight, and Isabel was making him describe to her the chulos, in their pale satin breeches and silk waist-scarfs; the toreros in their scarlet mantles; and the picadores on their horses.

"And I assure you," he said, "the company of ladies was very great and splendid. They were in full dress, and the golden-pinned mantillas and the sea of waving fans were a sight indeed. Oh, the fans alone! So many colors, Señorita Isabel, no one can imagine it."

"Oh, I assure you, Señor, I can see and feel it. But to be there! That, indeed, would make me perfectly happy."

"Had you been there today you would have admired, above all things, the feat of the matadore Jarocho. It was upon the great bull Sandoval—a very monster, I assure you. He came bellowing at Jarocho, as if he meant his instant death. His eyeballs were living fire; his nostrils steamed with fury. Well, then, at the precise moment, Jarocho put his slippered feet between his horns, and vaulted, light as a bird flies, over his back. Then Sandoval turned to him again. Well, he calmly waited for his approach, and his long sword met him between the horns. As lightly as a lady touches her cavalier, he seemed to touch Sandoval; but the brute fell like a stone at his feet. What a storm of vivas! What clapping of hands and shouts of 'valiente!' And the ladies flung their flowers, and the men flung their hats into the arena, and Jarocho stepped proudly enough on them, I can tell you, though he was watching the door for the next bull."

"Ah, Señor, why will men fight each other, when it is so much more grand and interesting to fight bulls?"

"Señorita Isabel, if you could only convince them of that! But then, it is not always interesting to the matadore. For instance, it is only by the mercy of God and the skill of an Americano that Jarocho is at this moment out of purgatory."

The Señora raised herself from among the satin pillows of her sofa, and asked, excitedly, "Was there then some accident, Señor? Is Jarocho wounded?"

"Not a hair of his head is hurt, Señora. I will tell you. Saint Jago, who followed Sandoval, was a little devil. He was light and quick, and he had intelligence. You could see by the gleam in his eyes that he took in the whole

scene and considered not only the people in the ring but
the people in the amphitheatre also to be his tormentors.
Perhaps in that reflection he was not mistaken. He
meant mischief from the beginning, and he pressed
Jarocho so close that he leaped the barrier for safety. As
he leaped, Saint Jago leaped also. Imagine now the terror
of the spectators! The screams! The rush! The lowered
horns within an inch of Jarocho, and Fray Joseph Maria
running with the consecrated wafer to the doomed man!
At that precise moment there was a rifle-shot, and the
bellowing brute rolled backward into the arena—dead."

"How grand! In such moments one really lives, Señor.
And but for this absurd rebellion I and my daughters
could have had the emotion. It is indeed cruel."

"You said the shot was fired by an American?"

"Señorita Antonia, it was, indeed. By Colonel
Crockett, himself."

Lopez rose and bowed to the ladies, and, as the
Señora was making some polite answer, the door of the
room opened quickly, and a man entered. Every eye was
turned on him, but ere a word could be uttered he was
kneeling at the Señora's side. In the dim light she knew
him at once, and she cried out: "Thomas! My Thomas!
My dear son! For three years I have not seen you."

He brought into the room with him an atmosphere
of comfort and strength. Suddenly all fear and anxiety
was lifted, and in Antonia's heart the reaction was so
great that she sank into a chair and began to cry like a
child. Her brother held her in his arms and soothed her
with the promise of his presence and help. Then he
said, cheerfully:

"Let me have some supper, Antonia. I am as hungry as a lobos wolf. Run away, Isabel, and help your sister, for I declare to you girls I shall eat everything in the house."

The homely duty was precisely what was needed to bring everyone's feelings to their normal condition. While his sisters prepared the meal, Thomas Worth sat chatting with his mother and Lopez of his father, and Jack, and Dare, and Luis, and the superficial events of the time.

In less than half an hour Antonia called her brother, and he and Lopez entered the dining-room together. They came in as brothers might come, but Antonia could not but notice the difference in the two men. Lopez was dressed in a suit of black velvet, trimmed with many small silver buttons. His sash was of crimson silk, his linen was richly embroidered, and his wide black-velvet hat was adorned with silver tags. It was a dress that set off admirably his dark, intelligent face.

Thomas Worth wore the usual frontier costume: a dark flannel shirt, a wide leather belt, buck-skin breeches, and leather boots covering his knees. He was very like his father in figure and face—darker, perhaps, and less handsome. But the gentleness and strength of his personal appearance attracted everyone first and invested all traits with their own distinctive charm.

What a change was there in the Señora's room. The poor lady cried a little for joy, and then went to sleep like a wearied child. Isabel and Antonia were too happy to sleep. They sat half through the night, talking softly of the danger they had been in. Now that Thomas had come, they could say *had*. They could even contemplate the expected visit of Fray Ignatius without fear; yes, indeed, with something very like satisfaction.

chapter **13**

The Arrival of Santa Anna

*L*eft to themselves, the two men threw off the mask of cheerfulness they had worn in the presence of the Señora. Thomas Worth ate heartily, for he had been without food since morning; but Navarro did not attempt to join his meal. He sat patiently waiting, his sombre eyes fixed upon the fire.

Presently Thomas Worth turned toward the hearth, and pushed the cedar logs on it to a focus. "Lopez," he said, "it strikes me that I am just in time to prevent some infamous plan of Fray Ignatius and my uncle Gonzaga."

"I should not have lost sight of the Señora and your sisters. I have watched them faithfully, though for many good reasons it has been best to appear indifferent. Will you now remain in San Antonio?"

"I have come with orders for Travis to blow up the Alamo and fall back upon Houston, who is at Gonzales. But I do not think the men will permit him to do so."

"You have too many leaders. Also, they undervalue the Mexican soldiers. I assure you they do. They fought Spain for ten years; they do not want, then, the persistence of true valor. The Americans may die in the Alamo, but they cannot hold it against the thousands Santa Anna will bring with him."

"They will die, then. They have no thought of retreat, nor of any deed that argues fear. Every man relies on himself, as if in his hand the moment of victory lay."

"Every man will perish."

"They will not perish in vain. Defeat is only a spur to the American soldier. Every one makes him a better fighter. If Santa Anna massacres the men in the Alamo, he seals the freedom of Texas."

"Houston should have come himself."

"Houston is biding his time. He is doing at present the hardest duty a great man can do: setting an example of obedience to a divided and incompetent government. Lopez, you said rightly that we had too many leaders. When those appointed for sacrifice have been offered up—when we are in the extremity of danger and ruin— then Houston will hear the word he is waiting for."

"And he will lead you on to victory. Indeed, I know it. I have seen him. He has the line—the fortunate line on the forehead. He is the loadstone in the breast of your cause. He will find a way or make a way for freedom."

Subsequent events proved the opinion of Thomas Worth correct with regard to the garrison in the Alamo. David Crockett! James Bowie! Barret Travis! The names were a host in themselves, and to a man they all refused to couple their names with retreat.

The same spirit moved every soul at Goliad. Fanning was there with nearly 900 men. He had named the place Fort Defiance, and he asserted his determination to hold it. In the meantime, Houston was using his great personal influence to collect troops, to make treaties with the Indians, and to keep together some semblance of a provisional government.

But it had become evident to all the leading spirits of the revolution that no half-way measures would now do. They only produced half-way enthusiasm. For this end, Houston had spoken out with his accustomed boldness:

"Gentlemen, we must declare the independence of Texas, and like our fore-elders, sink or swim by that declaration. Nothing else, nothing less, can save us. The planters of Texas must feel that they are fighting for their own constitution, and not for Mexican promises made to them twelve years ago and never yet kept."

The simple proposition roused a new enthusiasm, for while Urrea was hastening toward Goliad and Santa Anna toward San Antonio, the divided people were becoming more and more embittered. The American soldiers, who had hitherto gone in and out among the citizens of San Antonio during the day and only slept in the Alamo, were conscious of an ominous change in the temper of the city. They gathered their recruits together and shut themselves in the fortress.

Again Thomas Worth urged them to fall back either upon the line of Houston at Gonzales or Fanning at Goliad, but in the indecision and uncertainty of all official orders Crockett thought it best to make the first stand at the Mexican city.

"We can, at least," he said, "keep Santa Anna busy long enough to give the women and children of our own settlements time to escape, and the men time to draw together with a certain purpose."

"The cry of Santa Anna has been like the cry of wolf! wolf!" said Bowie. "I hear that great numbers that were under arms have gone home to plant their corn and cotton. Do you want Santa Anna to murder them piece-meal—house by house, family by family? Which of us would accommodate him with a prolonged pleasure like that? No! he shall have a square fight for every life he gets." And the calm, gentlemanly Bowie was suddenly transformed into a flashing, vehement, furious avenger.

"Gentlemen," answered Travis, "I go with Crockett and Bowie. If we hold the Alamo, it is a deed well done. If we fall with it, it is still a deed well done. We shall have given to Houston and Fanning time to interpose themselves between Santa Anna and the settlements."

"We have none of us lived very well," said Bowie, "but we can die well. I say as an American, that Texas is ours by right of natural locality, and by right of treaty; and, as I live, I will do my best to make it American by right of conquest! Comrades, I do not want a prettier quarrel to die in"—and looking with a brave, unflinching gaze around the grim fortress—"I do not want a better monu-ment than the Alamo!"

The speech was not answered with any noisy hurrah-ing, but the men around the long, bare table clasped hands across it. From that last interview with the doomed men Thomas Worth came away with the knowl-edge that he had seen the battle begun. He felt now that there was no time to delay longer his plans for the safety of his mother and sisters.

The day after his arrival he had begun to prepare, as far as possible, for this last emergency, but the Señora's unconquerable aversion to leave her native city had constantly hampered him. Until Santa Anna really appeared she would not believe in the necessity of such a movement. The proposal of Fray Ignatius, even if it did end in a convent, did not seem so terrible as to be a wanderer without a roof to cover her. She felt aggrieved and injured by Antonia's and Isabel's positive refusal to accept sanctuary from the priest, and with the underhand cunning of a weak woman she had contrived to let Fray Ignatius know that *she* was not to blame for the refusal.

All the same the priest hated her in conjunction with her children. On the morning after her interview with her uncle, he went to receive her submission; for the marquis had informed him of all that had passed, and he felt the three women and the valuable Worth property already under his hard hand. He opened the gate with the air of a proprietor. He looked down the lovely alleys of the garden, and up at the latticed stories of the handsome house, with that solid satisfaction which is the reward of what is acquired by personal effort or wisdom.

When he entered the door and was confronted by Thomas Worth, he was for the moment nonplussed. But he did not permit his confusion and disappointment to appear. He had not seen Thomas for a long time. He addressed him with suavity and regrets, and yet, "was

sure he would be glad to hear that, in the present dangerous crisis, the Marquis de Gonzaga had remembered the
blood-tie and offered his protection to a family so desolate."

Thomas Worth leaned upon the balusters, as if
guarding the approach to the Señora's apartments. He
answered: "The protection of the marquis is unnecessary. Three ladies are too great a charge for one so aged.
We will not impose it." The face of the young man was
calm and stern, but he spoke without visible temper,
until the priest prepared to pass him. Then he stretched
out his arm as a barrier.

"Fray Ignatius, you have already passed beyond the
threshold; permit me to remind you of Dr. Worth's words
on that subject."

"I put my duty before any man's words."

"Sir, for my mother's sake, I would not be disrespectful. But I assure you, also, that I will not permit any
man, while I live, to disregard my father's orders regarding his own household."

"I must see the Señora."

"That, I reply, is impossible."

"Presume not—dare not to interfere with a priest in
the duty of his office. It is a mortal sin. The curse of the
Church will rest upon you."

"The curse of the Church will not trouble me. But to
treat my father's known wishes with contempt—that is
an act of dishonor and disobedience which I will not be
guilty of."

"Santa Maria! Suffer not my spirit to be moved by
this wicked one. Out of my path, Satanas!"

The last word was not one which Thomas Worth had expected. He flushed crimson at its application, and with a few muttered sentences, intelligible only to the priest, he took him firmly by the shoulder, led him outside the door, and closed and barred it.

The expulsion was not accomplished without noisy opposition on the part of Fray Ignatius, and it pained Thomas deeply to hear, in the midst of the priest's anathemas, the shrill cries of his mother's distress and disapproval.

The next domestic movement of Thomas Worth was to rid the house of Molly and Manuel and the inferior servants. It was not as easy a task as may be supposed. They had been ordered by Fray Ignatius to remain, and the order had not been countermanded. Even if the Señora and her daughters were going east and their services were not needed, they had no objections to remain in the Worth house. They understood that the Church would take possession, and the housekeeping of the Church was notoriously easy and luxurious.

However, after exorbitant compensation had been made, and Molly had given in return "a bit of her mind," she left for the Irish colony of San Patricio, and Manuel immediately sought his favorite monte table. When he had doubled his money, he intended to obey Molly's emphatic orders, and go and tell the priest all about it.

"I would rather face a battery of cannon than Fray Ignatius and the servants again, Antonia." Antonia looked at her brother; he was worried and weary, and his first action, when he had finally cleared the house,

was to walk around it and bolt every door and window.
Antonia followed him silently. She perceived that the
crisis had come, and she was doing as good women in
extremity do—trying to find in the darkness the hand
always stretched out to guide and strengthen. As yet she
had not been able to grasp it. She followed her brother
like one in a troubled dream, whispering faintly, with
white lips, "O God, where art Thou? Help and pity us!"

Thomas led her finally to his father's office. He went
to a closet filled with drugs, removed them, and then a
certain pressure of his hand caused the back of the closet
to disappear in a groove, and a receptacle full of coin and
papers was disclosed.

"We must take with us all the coin we can carry.
What you are not likely to require is to go to the men in
the field. Then, hide in its place the old silver, and the
laces, and the jewels, which came with the Flores from
Castile; and any other papers and valuables, which you
received from our father. I think even Fray Ignatius will
not discover them here."

"Is there any special need to hurry today?

"Santa Anna is within forty-eight hours of San Antonio. He may force a march and arrive earlier. Travis told
me last night that their advance scouts had come in with
this intelligence. Today they will gather every man they
can and prepare to defend themselves in the Alamo. As
soon as Santa Anna arrives, we are in danger. I must
leave here tonight. I must either take you with me or
remove you to a place of more safety."

"Let us go with you."

"If my mother is willing."

"If she is not, what then?"

"Lopez has prepared for that emergency. He has an empty house three miles west of San Antonio. He has had it completely victualed. I will take you there after dark in the large green chariot. Ortiz will drive the light Jersey wagon on the Gonzales road. When inquiry is made, the Jersey wagon will have attracted the attention of every Mexican, and Fray Ignatius will receive positive assurances that you were in it and are beyond his power. And certainly, without definite intelligence, he would never suspect you of being anywhere on the highway to Mexico."

"Shall we be alone?"

"For two or three days you will be quite alone. Ortiz will, however, return with the wagon by a circuitous route; for, sooner or later, you are sure to need it. Fear not to trust him. Only in one respect will you need to supplement his advice by your own intelligence: he is so eager to fight Santa Anna, he may persuade himself and you that it is necessary to fly eastward when it is not. In all other points you may be guided by him. His disguise as a peasant is so perfect that it will be easy for him to gather in the pulquerias all the information requisite for your direction. I have been out to the house, and I can assure you that Lopez has considered everything for your comfort."

"I would rather go with you, Thomas."

"It must be as mother desires."

When the circumstances were explained to the Señora, she was at first very determined to accept neither alternative. 'She would remain where she was. She was a Flores and a Gonzaga. Santa Anna knew better than to molest her. She would rather trust to him than to those dreadful Americans.' Reminded of Fray Ignatius, she shed a few tears over the poor padrecito, and assured her children they had made a mistake regarding him, which neither oil nor ointment, nor wit nor wisdom, could erase.

It was almost impossible to induce her to come to a decision of any kind. Only when she saw Antonia and Isabel were dressed for a journey, and that Thomas had locked up all the rooms and was extinguishing the fires, could she bring herself to believe that the trial so long anticipated had really come.

"My dearest mother! My own life and the lives of many others may now hang upon a few moments. I can remain here no longer. Where shall I take you to?"

"I will not leave my home."

"Santa Anna is almost here. As soon as he arrives, Fray Ignatius and twelve of the Bernardine monks are coming here. I was told that yesterday."

"Then I will go to the convent. I and my daughters."

"No, mother. If you go to the convent, Antonia and Isabel must go with me."

She prayed, exclaimed, and appealed to saints and angels until Isabel was hysterically weeping, Antonia at a mental tension almost unendurable, and Thomas on the verge of one of those terrifying passions that mark the extremity of habitually gentle, patient men.

"Mother, there is no time to deliberate!" he exclaimed with a stamp of his spurred boot on the stone floor. "If you will go to the priests, you must go alone. Kiss your mother farewell, girls. I have not another moment to wait."

Then, in a passion of angry sobs and reproaches, she decided to go with her daughters, and no saints ever suffered with a more firm conviction of their martyrdom to duty than did this poor foolish, affectionate slave to her emotions and her superstitions. But when Thomas had gone, and nothing was to be gained by a display of her sufferings, she permitted herself to be interested in their hiding place. And after Antonia had given her a cup of chocolate, and Isabel had petted and soothed her, she began gradually to allow them to explain their situation, and even to feel some interest in its discussion.

They sat in the dusky glimmer of starlight, for candles and fire were forbidden luxuries. Fortunately, the weather was warm and sunny, and for making chocolate and such simple cookery, Lopez had provided a spirit lamp. The Señora was as pleased as a child with this arrangement. She had never seen anything like it before. She even imagined that the food cooked upon it had some rare and unusual flavor. She was quite proud when she had learned its mysteries, and quite sure that chocolate she made upon it was chocolate of a most superior kind.

The house had been empty for two years, and the great point was to preserve its air of desolation. No outside arrangement was touched; the torn remnants of some balcony hangings were left fluttering in the wind; the closed windows and the closed doors, the absence of smoke from the chimneys and of lights from the win-

dows, preserved the air of emptiness and loneliness that
the passers-by had been accustomed to see. And, as it
was on the highway into the city, there were great numbers of passers: mule-trains going to Mexico and
Sonora; cavaliers and pedestrians; splendidly dressed
nobles and officials; dusty peasants bringing in wood;
ranchmen, peddlers, and the whole long list of the great
city's purveyors and servants. Isabel took cushions up on
the flat roof, and lying down, watched, from between the
pilasters of the balustrade surrounding it, the moving
panorama.

On the morning of the third day of what the Señora
called their *imprisonment*, they went to the roof to sit in
the clear sunshine and the fresh wind. They were weary
and depressed with the loneliness and uncertainty of
their position, and were almost longing for something to
happen that would push forward the lagging wheels of
destiny.

A long fanfare of trumpets, a roll of drums, a stirring
march of warlike melody, startled them out of the lethar-
gic tedium of exhausted hopes and fears. "It is Santa
Anna!" said Antonia; and though they durst not stand up,
they drew closer to the balustrade and watched for the
approaching army. Antonia was still and speechless, and
white as death. Isabel watched with gleaming eyes and
set lips. The Señora's excitement was unmistakably that
of exultant national pride.

Santa Anna and his staff-officers were in front. They
passed too rapidly for individual notice, but it was a
grand moving picture of handsome men in scarlet and
gold—of graceful mangas, waving plumes, and bright-

colored velvet capes; of high-mettled horses, with richly adorned Mexican saddles, aqueras of black fur, and silver stirrups; of thousands of common soldiers in a fine uniform of red and blue, with antique brazen helmets gleaming in the sun and long lances adorned with tri-colored streamers. They went past like a vivid, wonderful dream—like the vision of an army of medieval knights.

In a few minutes, the tumult of the advancing army was increased tenfold by the clamor of the city pouring out to meet it. The clashing bells from the steeples, the shouting of the populace, the blare of trumpets and roll of drums, the lines of churchmen and officials in their grandest dresses, of citizens of every age—the indescribable human murmur—altogether it was a scene whose sensuous splendor obliterated for a time the capacity of impressionable natures to judge rightly.

But Antonia saw beyond all this brave show the cruel reality of war, and her eyes grew dim, and her heart rose in pitying prayer for that small band of heroes standing together for life and liberty in the grim Alamo. No pomp or parade was theirs. They were isolated from all their fellows. They were surrounded by their enemies. No word of sympathy could reach them. Yet she knew they would stand like lions at bay; they would give life to its last drop for liberty. Rather than be less than freemen, they would prefer not to be at all.

chapter **14**

The Fall of the Alamo

*T*he passing-by of Santa Anna and the Mexican army, though it had been hourly expected for nearly three days, was an event which threw the Señora and her daughters into various conditions of mental excitement. They descended from the roof to the Señora's room, where they could move about and converse with more freedom. The poor lady was quite unable to control her speech and actions, and she was also much irritated by Antonia's more composed manner. She thought it was want of sympathy.

"How can you take things with such a blessed calmness," she asked, angrily. "But it is the way of the Americans, no doubt, who must have everything for prudence. Sensible! Sensible! Sensible! that is the tune they are forever playing, and you dance to it like a miracle."

"My dear mother, can we do any good by exclaiming and weeping?"

"Perhaps not; but to have a little human nature is more agreeable to those who are yet on the earth side of purgatory."

"Mi madre," said Isabel, "Antonia is our good angel. She thinks for us, and plans for us, and even now has everything ready for us to move at a moment's notice. Our good angels have to be sensible and prudent, madre."

"To move at a moment's notice! Where shall we go to? Could my blessed father and mother see me in this prison, this very vault, I assure you they would be unhappy even among the angels."

"Mother, there are hundreds of women today in Texas who would think this house a palace of comfort and safety."

"Saints and angels! Is that my fault? Does it make my condition more endurable? Ah, my children, I have seen great armies come into San Antonio, and always before I have been able to make a little pleasure to myself out of the event. If we were only in our own home! It must have been the devil who made us leave it."

"How truly splendid the officers looked, mi madre. I dare say Señora Valdez will entertain them."

"That is certain. And as for Dorette Valdez—the coquette[44]—it will certainly be a great happiness to her."

Isabel sighed, and the Señora felt a kind of satisfaction in the sigh. It was unendurable to be alone in her regrets and her longings.

"Yes," she continued, "every night Señora Trespalacios will give a tertulia, and the officers will have military balls. The brave young men—they will be so gay, so charming, so devoted, and in a few hours, perhaps, they will go into the other world by the road of the battlefield. Ah, how pitiful! But how interesting! Cannot you imagine it?"

---

[44]coquette [kō·kĕt′]—flirt

Isabel sighed again, but the sigh was for the gay, the charming Luis Alveda. When she thought of him, she forgot in a moment to envy Dorette Valdez and the señoritas of the noble house of Trespalacios. Some sudden, swift touch of sympathy made the Señora at the same moment remember her husband and her sons, and an anxious sorrow drove out all smaller annoyances. Then both she and her daughters wept together, until their community of grief had brought to each heart the solemn strength of a divine hope and reliance.

"My children, I will go now and pray," said the sorrowful wife and mother. "At the foot of the cross I will wait for the hour of deliverance." And casting herself on her knees, with her crucifix in her hand, she appeared in a moment to have forgotten everything but her anguish and her sins, and the Lamb of God upon whom, with childlike faith, she was endeavoring to cast them.

That night, when all was dark and still, Ortiz returned with the wagon. In the morning Antonia went to speak to him. He looked worn-out and sorrowful, and she feared to ask him for news. "There is food in the house, and I have made you chocolate," she said, as she scanned the man's exhausted condition with pity.

"The Señorita is kind as the angels. I will eat and drink at her order. I am, indeed, faint and hungry."

She brought him to the table, and when he refused to sit in her presence, she said frankly, "Captain Ortiz, you are our friend and not our servant. Rest and refresh yourself."

He bent upon one knee and kissed the hand she offered, and without further remonstrance obeyed her

desire. Isabel came in shortly and with the tact of true
kindness she made no remark, but simply took the chair
beside Ortiz, and said, in her usual voice and manner:
"Good morning, Captain. We are glad to see you. Did
you meet my brother Thomas again?"

"Señorita, God be with you! I have not seen him. I
was at Goliad."

"Then you would see our brother Juan?"

"Si. The Señor Juan is in good health and great
happiness. He sent by my willing hands a letter."

"Perhaps also you saw his friend, Señor Grant?"

"From him, also, I received a letter. Into your gracious care, Señorita, I deliver them."

"I thank you for your kindness, Captain. Tell us now
of the fortress. Are the troops in good spirits?"

"Allow me to fear that they are in too good assurance
of success. Most of the men are very young. They have
promised to themselves the independence of Texas.
They will also conquer Mexico. There are kingdoms in
the moon for them. I envy such exaltations—and regret
them. My heart ached to see the crowds of bright young
faces. With a Napoleon—with a Washington to lead
them—they would do miracles."

"What say you to Houston?"

"I know him not. At Goliad they are all Houstons.
They believe each man in himself. On the contrary, I
wish that each man looked to the same leader."

"Do you know that Santa Anna is in San Antonio?"

"I felt it, though I had no certain news. I came far
around and hid myself from all passers-by, for the sake
of the wagon and the horses. I have the happiness to say

they are safe. The wagon is within the enclosure, the
horses are on the prairie. They have been well trained,
and will come to my call. As for me, I will now go into
the city, for there will be much to see and to hear that
may be important to us. Señoritas, for all your desires, I
am at your service."

When Ortiz was gone, Isabel had a little fret of disappointment. Luis might have found some messenger to
bring her a word of his love and life. What was love
worth that did not annihilate impossibilities! However, it
consoled her a little to carry Jack's letter to his mother.
The Señora had taken her morning chocolate and fallen
asleep. When Isabel awakened her, she opened her eyes
with a sigh and a look of hopeless misery. These pallid
depressions attacked her most cruelly in the morning,
when the room, shabby and unfamiliar, gave both her
memory and anticipation a shock.

But the sight of the letter flushed her face with expectation. She took it with smiles. She covered it with
kisses. When she opened it, a curl from Jack's head fell
on to her lap. She pressed it to her heart, and then rose
and laid it at the feet of her Madonna.[45] "She must share
my joy," she said with a pathetic childishness. "She will
understand it." Then, with her arm around Isabel, and
the girl's head on her shoulder, they read together Jack's
loving words:

"Mi madre, you have Juan's heart in your heart. Believe me, that in all this trouble I sorrow only for you.
When victory is won I shall fly to you. Other young

---

[45]Madonna—a statue of Mary, the mother of Jesus

men have other loves; I have only you, sweet mother.
There is always the cry in my heart for the kiss I
missed when I left you. If I could hold your hand tonight, if I could hear your voice, I would say that the
Holy One had given me the best blessings He had in
heaven. Send to me a letter, madre—Forgive Juan!
Think of this only: HE IS MY BOY! If I live, it is for
you, who are the loveliest and dearest of mothers. If I
die, I shall die with your name on my lips. Mi madre,
remember me! In your prayers, remember Juan!"

With tears and sobs the letter was read by all the
women, and the Señora finally laid it where she had laid
the precious curl that had come with it. She wanted "the
Woman blessed among women" to share the mother joy
and the mother anguish in her heart. Besides, she was a
little nervous about Jack's memento of himself. Her
superstitious lore taught her that severed hair is a token
of severed love. She wished he had not sent it, and yet
she could not bear to have it out of her sight.

"I have one child that loves me and me only. I shall
forgive Juan everything. I shall not forgive Thomas many
things. But Juan! oh! it is impossible not to love him
entirely. There is no one like him in the world. If the
good God will only give him back to me, I will say a
prayer of thanks every day of my life long. Oh, Juan!
Juan! my dear boy!"

Jack's letter brightened the day and formed a new
topic of conversation, until Ortiz returned in the evening.
His disguise had enabled him to linger about the Plaza
and monte table, and to hear and observe all that was
going on.

"The city is enjoying itself and making money," he said, in reply to question from the Señora. "Certainly the San Antonians approve of liberty, but what would you do? In Rome one does not quarrel with the Pope; in San Antonio one must approve of despotism, when Santa Anna parades himself there."

"Has he made any preparations for attacking the Alamo? Will the Americans resist him?"

"Señorita Antonia, he is erecting a battery on the river bank, three hundred yards from the Alamo. This morning, ere the ground was touched, he reviewed his men in the Plaza. He stood on an elevation at the church door, surrounded by his officers and the priests, and unfurled the Mexican flag."

"That was about eleven o'clock, Captain?"

"Si, Señorita. Why do you ask?"

"I heard at that hour a dull roar of human voices—a roar like nothing on earth but the distant roar of the ocean."

"To be sure—it was the shouting of the people. When all was still, Fray Ignatius blessed the flag and sprinkled over it holy water. Then Santa Anna raised it to his lips and kissed it. Another shout. Then he crossed his sword upon the flag, and he cried out—'Soldados![46] you are here to defend this banner, which is the emblem of your holy faith and of your native land, against heretics, infidels, and ungrateful traitors. Do you swear to do it?' And the whole army answered 'Si! si! juramos!'[47] Again

---

[46]Soldados [sôl·däd′ôs]—soldiers
[47]Si! juramos! [sē hōōr′ä·môs]—Yes, we swear!

he kissed the flag, and laid his sword across it, and there was another shout. It was a very clever thing, I assure you, Señora, and it sent every soldier to the battery with a great heart."

The Señora's easily touched feelings were all on fire at the description. "I wish I could have seen the blessing of the banner," she said. "It is a ceremony to fill the soul. I have always wept at it. Mark, Antonia! This confirms what I assured you of—the Mexicans make war with a religious feeling and a true refinement. And pray, Captain Ortiz, how will the Americans oppose these magnificent soldiers, full of piety and patriotism?"

"They have the Alamo, and one hundred and eighty-three men in it."

"And four thousand men against them?"

"Si. An urgent appeal for assistance was sent to Fanning at Goliad. Señor Navarro took it on a horse fleet as the wind."

"Will Fanning answer the appeal?"

"If the answer be permitted him. But Urrea may prevent. Also other things."

Santa Anna entered San Antonio on Tuesday the twenty-third of February, 1836, and by the twenty-seventh the siege had become a very close one. Entrenched encampments encircled the doomed men in the Alamo, and from dawn to sunset the bombardment went on. The tumult of the fight—the hurrying in and out of the city—the clashing of church bells between the booming of cannon—these things the Señora and her daughters could hear and see; but all else was for twelve days mere surmise. But only one surmise was possible, when it was

known that the little band of defiant heroes were fighting twenty times their own number—that no help could
come to them—that the Mexicans were cutting off their
water, and that their provisions were getting very low.
The face of Ortiz grew constantly more gloomy, and yet
there was something of triumph in his tone as he told
the miserably anxious women with what desperate valor
the Americans were fighting, and how fatally every one
of their shots told.

On Saturday night, the fifth of March, he called
Antonia aside, and said, "My Señorita, you have a great
heart, and so I speak to you. The end is close. Today
the Mexicans succeeded in getting a large cannon within
gunshot of the Alamo, just where it is weakest. Señor
Captain Crockett has stood on the roof all day, and as
the gunners have advanced to fire it he has shot them
down. A group of Americans were around him; they
loaded rifles and passed them to him as quickly as he
could fire them. Santa Anna was in a fury past believ-
ing. He swore then 'by every saint in heaven or hell' to
enter the Alamo tomorrow. Señor Navarro says he is
raging like a tiger, and that none of his officers dare
approach him. The Señor bade me tell you that tomorrow night he will be here to escort you to Gonzales. For
no American will his fury spare, and he knows neither
sex nor age in his passions. When the Alamo falls, the
soldiers will spread themselves around for plunder, or
shelter, and this empty house is sure to attract them.
The Señorita sees with her own intelligence how things
must take place."

"I understand, Captain. Will you go with us?"

"I will have the Jersey wagon ready at midnight. I know the horses. Before sun-up we shall have made many miles."

That night as Antonia and her sister sat in the dark together, Antonia said: "Isabel, tomorrow the Alamo will fall. There is no hope for the poor, brave souls there. Then Santa Anna will kill every American."

"Oh, Antonia, what is to become of us? We shall have no home, nothing to eat, nowhere to sleep. I think we shall die. Also, there is mi madre. How I do pity her!"

"She is to be your care, Isabel. I shall rely on you to comfort and manage her. I will attend to all else. We are going to our father and Thomas—and Luis."

"Yes, and after all I am very tired of this dreadful life. It is a kind of convent. One is buried alive here, and still not safe. Do you really imagine that Luis is with my father and Thomas?"

"I feel sure of it."

"What a great enjoyment it will be for me to see him again!"

"And how delighted he will be! And as it is necessary that we go, Isabel, we must make the best of the necessity. Try and get mi madre to feel this."

"I can do that with a few words, and tears, and kisses. Mi madre is like one's good angel—very easy to persuade."

"And now we must try and sleep, queridita."

"Are you sure there is no danger tonight, Antonia?"

"Not tonight. Say your prayer, and sleep in God's presence. There is yet nothing to fear. Ortiz and Lopez Navarro are watching every movement."

But early in the morning, the quiet of their rest was broken by sharp bugle calls. The stars were yet in the sky, and all was so still that they thrilled the air like something unearthly. Antonia started up, and ran to the roof. Bugle was answering bugle, and their tones were imperative and cruel.

In wild, savage gusts, she heard the military bands playing the infamous Dequelo, whose notes of blood and fire commingled shrieked in every ear—"NO QUARTER! NO QUARTER!" A prolonged shout, the booming of cannon, an awful murmurous tumult, a sense of horror, of crash and conflict, answered the merciless, frenzied notes, and drowned them in the shrieks and curses they called for.

It was yet scarcely dawn. Her soul, moved by influences so various and so awful, became almost rebellious. Why did God permit such cruelties? Did He know? Would He allow a handful of men to be overpowered by numbers? Being omnipotent, would He not in some way, at least, make the fight equal? As she went about the simple preparations for their breakfast, she wept continuously— tears of indignation and sorrow—tears coming from the strength of feeling, rather than its weakness. The Señora could eat nothing. Isabel was white with terror. They wandered from window to window in the last extremity of anxiety.

About seven o'clock they saw Ortiz pass the house. There were so many people on the road he could not find an opportunity to enter for some time. He had been in the city all night. He had watched the movement of the troops in the starlight. As he drank a cup of chocolate, he said:

"It was just three o'clock, Señorita, when the Matamoras battalion was moved forward. General Cos supported it with two thousand men."

"But General Cos was paroled by these same Americans who are now in the Alamo. His life was spared on condition that he would not bear arms against them again."

"It is but one lie, one infamy more. When I left the city, about four thousand men were attacking the Alamo. The infantry, in columns, were driven up to the walls by the cavalry which surrounded them."

"The Americans! Is there any hope for them?"

"The mercy of God remains, Señorita. That is all. The Alamo is not as the everlasting hills. What men have made, men can also destroy. Señor Navarro is in the church, praying for the souls that are passing every moment."

"He ought to have been fighting. To help the living is better than to pray for the dead."

"Permit me to assure you, Señorita Antonia, that no man has done more for the living. In time of war, there must be many kinds of soldiers. Señor Navarro has given nearly all that he possesses for the hope of freedom. And he has done secret service of incalculable value."

"Secret service! I prefer those who have the courage of their convictions, and who stand by them publicly."

"This is to be considered, Señorita. But the man who can be silent can also speak when the day for speaking arrives." No one opposed this statement. It did not seem worth while to discuss opinions while the terrible facts of the position were appealing to every sense.

As the day went on, the conflict evidently became closer and fiercer. Ortiz went back to the city, and the three lonely women knelt upon the housetop, listening in terror to the tumult of the battle. About noon the firing ceased, and an awful silence—a silence that made the ears ache to be relieved of it—followed.

"All is over!" moaned Antonia, and she covered her face with her hands and sobbed bitterly. Isabel had already exhausted tears. The Señora, with her crucifix in her hand, was praying for the poor unfortunates dying without prayer.

During the afternoon, smoke and flame, and strange, sickening odors were blown northward of the city, and for some time it seemed probable that a great conflagration would follow the battle. How they longed for someone to come! The utmost of their calamity would be better than the intolerable suspense. But hour after hour went past, and not even Ortiz arrived. They began to fear that both he and Navarro had been discovered in some disloyalty and slain, and Antonia was heartsick when she considered the helplessness of their situation.

Still, in accordance with Navarro's instructions, they dressed for the contemplated journey, and sat in the dark, anxiously listening for footsteps. About eleven o'clock Navarro and Ortiz came together. Ortiz went for the horses, and Navarro sat down beside the Señora. She asked him, in a low voice, what had taken place, and he answered:

"Everything dreadful, everything cruel, and monstrous, and inhuman! Among the angels in heaven there is sorrow and anger this night." His voice had in it all the pathos of tears, but tears mingled with a burning indignation.

"The Alamo has fallen!"

"Señorita Antonia, I would give my soul to undo this day's work. It is a disgrace to Mexico which centuries cannot wipe out."

"The Americans?"

"Are all with the Merciful One."

"Not one saved?"

"Not one."

"Impossible!"

"I will tell you. It is right to tell the whole world such an infamy. If I had little children I would take them on my knee and teach them the story. I heard it from the lips of one wet-shod with their blood, dripping crimson from the battle—my own cousin, Xavier. He was with General Castrillon's division. They began their attack at four in the morning, and after two hours' desperate fighting succeeded in reaching a courtyard of the Alamo.

"They found the windows and doors barricaded with bags of earth. Behind these the Americans fought hand to hand with despairing valor. Ramires, Siesma, and Batres led the columns, and Santa Anna gave the signal of battle from a battery near the bridge. When the second charge was driven back, he became furious. He put himself in front of the men, and with shouts and oaths led them to the third charge. Xavier said that he inspired them with his own frenzy. They reached the foot of the wall, and the ladders were placed in position. The officers fell to the rear and forced the men to ascend them. As they reached the top they were stabbed, and the ladders overturned. Over and over again these attempts were made, until the garrison in the Alamo were exhausted with the struggle."

Navarro paused a few minutes, overpowered by his emotions. No one spoke. He could see Antonia's face, white as a spirit's in the dim light. Isabel was weeping, and the Señora had taken his hand.

"At last, at the hour of ten, the outer wall was gained. Then, room by room was taken with slaughter incredible. There were fourteen Americans in the hospital. They fired their rifles and pistols from their pallets with such deadly aim that Milagros turned a cannon upon them. They were blown to pieces, but at the entrance of the door they left forty dead Mexicans."

"Ah Señor, Señor! tell me no more. My heart cannot endure it."

"Mi madre," answered Isabel, "we must hear it all. Without it, one cannot learn to hate Santa Anna sufficiently," and her small, white teeth snapped savagely, as she touched the hand of Lopez with an imperative "Proceed."

"Colonel Bowie was helpless in bed. Two Mexican officers fired at him, and one ran forward to stab him ere he died. The dying man caught his murderer by the hair of his head, and plunged his knife into his heart. They went to judgment at the same moment."

"I am glad of it! Glad of it!" declared the Señora. "The American would say to the Almighty: 'Thou gavest me life, and thou gavest me freedom; freedom, that is the nobler gift of the two. This man robbed me of both.' And God is just. The Judge of the whole earth will do right."

"At noon, only six of the one hundred and eighty-three were left alive. They were surrounded by Castrillon and his soldiers. Xavier says his general was penetrated with admiration for these heroes. He spoke sympathizingly to Crockett, who stood in an angle of the fort, with his shattered rifle in his right hand, and his massive knife, dripping with blood, in his left. His face was gashed, his white hair crimson with blood; but a score of Mexicans, dead and dying, were around him. At his side was Travis, but so exhausted that he was scarcely alive.

"Castrillon could not kill these heroes. He asked their lives of Santa Anna, who stood with a scowling, savage face in this last citadel of his foes. For answer, he turned to the men around him, and said, with a malignant emphasis: 'Fire!' It was the last volley. Of the defenders of the Alamo, not one is left."

A solemn silence followed. For a few minutes it was painful in its intensity. Isabel broke it. She spoke in a whisper, but her voice was full of intense feeling. "I wish indeed the whole city had been burnt up. There was a fire this afternoon; I would be glad if it were burning yet."

"May God pardon us all, Señorita! That was a fire which does not go out. It will burn for ages. I will explain myself. Santa Anna had the dead Americans put into ox-wagons and carried to an open field outside the city. There they were burnt to ashes. The glorious pile was still casting lurid flashes and shadows as I passed it."

"I will hear no more! I will hear no more!" cried the Señora. "And I will go away from here. Ah, Señor, why do you not make haste? In a few hours we shall have daylight again. I am in a terror. Where is Ortiz?"

"He is calling the horses—there is the roll of the wagon on the flagged court. All, then, is ready. Señora, show now that you are of a noble house, and in this hour of adversity be brave, as the Flores have always been."

She was pleased by the entreaty, and took his arm with a composure which, though assumed, was a sort of strength. She entered the wagon with her daughters, and uttered no word of complaint. Then Navarro locked the gate, and took his seat beside Ortiz. The prairie turf deadened the beat of their horses' hoofs; they went at a flying pace, and when the first pallid light of morning touched the east, they had left San Antonio far behind and were nearing the beautiful banks of the Cibolo.

chapter **15**

Goliad

*N*ear midnight, on March the ninth, the weary
fugitives arrived at Gonzales. They had been
detained by the deep mud in the bottom lands, and by
the extreme exhaustion of the ladies, demanding some
hours' rest each day. The village was dark and quiet.
Here and there the glimmer of a candle, now and then
the call of a sentry, or the wail of a child broke the myste-
rious silence.

Ortiz appeared to know the ground perfectly. He
drove without hesitation to a log house in which a faint
thread of light was observable, and as he approached it
he gave a long, peculiar whistle. The door was instantly
thrown open, and, as the wagon stopped, two men
stepped eagerly to it. In another instant the Señora was
weeping in her husband's arms, and Isabel was laughing
and crying at Luis's side. When their wraps had been
removed from the wagon, Ortiz drove away, leaving
Navarro and Antonia standing by the little pile of ladies'
luggage.

"I will take charge of all, Señorita. Alas! How weary
you are!"

"It is nothing, Señor. Let me thank you for your great
kindness."

"Señorita, to be of service to you is my good fortune. If it were necessary, my life for your life, and I would die happy."

She had given him her hand with her little speech of thanks, and he raised it to his lips. It was an act of homage that he might have offered to a saint, but in it Lopez unconsciously revealed to Antonia the secret love in his heart. For he stood in the glow of light from the open door, and his handsome face showed, as in a glass darkly, the tenderness and hopelessness of his great affection. She was touched by the discovery, and though she had a nature faithful as the sunrise she could not help a feeling of kindly interest in one so reticent, so watchful, so forgetful of himself.

The log cabin in which they found shelter was at least a resting-place. A fire of cedar logs burned upon the hearth, and there was a bed in the room, and a few rude chairs covered with raw hide. But the Señora had a happy smile on her weary face. She ignored the poverty of her surroundings. She had her Roberto, and, for this hour at least, had forgiven fate.

Presently the coffeepot was boiling, and Doctor Worth and Luis brought out their small store of corn-bread and their tin camp-cups, and the weary women ate and drank, and comforted themselves in the love and protection at their side. Doctor Worth sat by his wife, and gave Antonia his hand. Isabel leaned her pretty head against Luis, and listened with happy smiles to his low words.

No one heeded their pretty, extravagant talk. It was a thing apart from the more serious interests discussed by Doctor Worth and his wife and eldest daughter. And when

Ortiz and Navarro joined the circle, the story of the fall of the Alamo was told again, and Luis forgot his own happiness and wept tears of anger and pity for the dead heroes.

"This brutal massacre was on the morning of the sixth, you say, Navarro?"

"Last Sabbath morning, Señor. Mass was being offered in the churches, and Te Deums sung while it went on."

"A mass to the devil it was," said Ortiz.

"Now, I will tell you something. On the morning of the second, Thomas was in Washington. A convention sitting there declared, on that day, the independence of Texas, and fifty-five out of fifty-six votes elected General Houston Commander-in-Chief."

"Houston! That is the name of victory! Gracias a Dios!"[48] cried Navarro.

"It is probable that the news of this movement influenced Santa Anna to such barbarity."

"It is his nature to be brutal."

"True, Ortiz; yet I can imagine how this proclamation would incense him. On the morning of the sixth, the convention received the last express sent by poor Travis from the Alamo. It was of the most thrilling character, breathing the very spirit of patriotism and courage—and despair. In less than an hour, Houston, with a few companions, was on his way to the Alamo. At the same time he sent an express to Fanning, urging him to meet him on the Cibolo. Houston will be here tomorrow."

---

[48]Gracias a Dios! [grä′sē·äs ä dē′ŏs]—Thanks be to God!

"Then he will learn that all help is too late."

But Houston had learned it in his own way before he reached Gonzales; for Travis had stated that as long as the Alamo could be held, signal guns would be fired at sunrise, and it is a well-authenticated fact that these guns could be heard by trained ears for more than one hundred miles across the prairie. Houston, whose senses were keen as the Indians with whom he had long lived, knew when he was within reach of the sound. He rose early and with his ear close to the ground waited in intense anxiety for the dull, rumbling murmur which would tell him the Alamo still held out. His companions stood at some distance, still as statues, intently watching him. The sun rose. He had listened in vain; not the faintest sound did his ear detect.

"The Alamo has fired its last gun," he said, on rejoining his companions.

"And the men, General?"

"They have died like men. You may be sure of that."

At Gonzales he heard the particulars, and he saw that the news had exerted a depressing influence upon the troops there. He called them together. He spoke to them of the brutal tragedy, and he invested its horrors with the grandeur of eternal purpose and the glory of heroic sacrifice.

"They were soldiers," he cried; "and they died like soldiers. Their names will be the morning stars of American history. They will live forever in the red monument of the Alamo." He looked like a lion, with a fierce stare his eyes commanded all he viewed. "Vengeance remains to us! We have declared our independence, and it must be maintained."

He immediately sent off another express to Fanning, apprising him of the fall of the Alamo and ordering him to blow up Goliad and fall back upon Gonzales. Then he sent wagons into the surrounding country to transport the women and children to the eastern settlements, for he knew well what atrocities would mark every mile of Santa Anna's progress through the country.

These wagons, with their helpless loads, were to rendezvous at Peach Creek, ten miles from Gonzales; where also he expected Fanning and his 860 men to join him. This addition would make the American force nearly 1,200 strong. Besides which, Fanning's little army was of the finest material, being composed mostly of enthusiastic volunteers from Georgia and Alabama. They were young men, who, like Dare Grant and John Worth, were inspired with the idea of freedom, or the spread of Americanism, or the fanaticism of religious liberty of conscience—perhaps, even, with hatred of priestly domination. Houston felt that he would be sufficient for Santa Anna when the spirit of this company was added to the moral force of men driven from their homes and families to fight for the lands they had bought and the rights which had been guaranteed them.

So he watched the horizon anxiously for Fanning's approach, often laying his ear to the ground to listen for what he could not see. And, impatient as he was for their arrival, the Señora was more so. She declared that her sufferings would be unendurable but for this hope. The one question on her lips, the one question in her eyes, was, "Are they coming?" And Antonia, though she did not speak of her private hopes, was equally anxious. To

have the whole family together would be in itself a great
help. Whatever their deprivations and fatigues, they
could comfort each other with their affection.

Every day wagon-loads of women and children
joined the camp, and the march eastward was very slow.
But no circumstance extols more loudly the bravery and
tenderness of these American soldiers than the patience
with which this encumbrance was endured. Men worn
out with watching and foraging were never too weary to
help some mother still more weary, or to carry some
little child whose swollen feet would no longer aid it.

One night they rested at a little place on the Colorado. In one room of a deserted cabin Houston sat with
Major Hockly, dictating to him a military dispatch. They
had no candles, and Houston was feeding the fire with
oak splinters, to furnish light enough for their necessity.
In the other room, the Worth family were gathered.
Antonia, in preparing for their journey, had wisely laid a
small mattress and a couple of pillows in the wagon; and
upon this mattress the Señora and Isabel were resting.
Doctor Worth and Thomas sat by the fire talking of
Fanning's delay, while Antonia was making some corn-
meal cakes for their supper.

When the Señora's portion was given to her she put
it aside and lifted her eyes to Antonia's face. They asked
the question forever in her heart, "Is Jack coming?" and
Antonia pitifully shook her head.

Then the poor woman seemed to have reached the
last pitch of endurance. "Let me die!" she cried. "I can
bear life no longer." To Mary and the saints she appealed with a passionate grief that was distressing to

witness. All the efforts of her husband and her children failed to soothe her and, as often happens in a complication of troubles, she seized upon the most trifling as the text of her complaint.

"I cannot eat corn bread; I have always detested it. I am hungry. I am perishing for my chocolate. And I have no clothing—I am ashamed of myself. I thank the saints I have no looking-glass. Oh, Roberto! What have you done to your Maria?"

"My dear wife! Be patient a little longer. Think, love, you are not alone. There are women here far more weary, far more hungry—several who, in the confusion, have lost their little children, and others who are holding dying babes in their arms."

"Giver of all good! give me patience. I have to say to you that other women's sorrows do not make me grateful for my own. And Santa Maria has been cruel to me. Another more cruel, who can find? I have confessed to her my heartache about Juan; entreated her to bring my boy to me. Has she done it?"

"My darling Maria."

"It is now the twenty-third of March; I have been seventeen days wandering with my daughters like very beggars. If only I had had the discretion to remain in my own house!"

"Maria, Lopez will tell you that Fray Ignatius and the brothers are in possession of it. He saw them walking about the garden reading their breviaries."

At this moment General Houston, in the opposite room was dictating: "Before God, I have found the darkest hours of my life. For forty-eight hours I have neither eaten an ounce of anything, nor have I slept." The Señora's sobbing troubled him. He rose to close the door, and saw two men entering. One leaned upon the other and appeared to be at the point of death.

"Where is there a doctor, General?"

"In that room, sir. Have you brought news of Fanning?"

"I have."

"Leave your comrade with the doctor, and report."

The entrance of the wounded man silenced the Señora. She turned her face to the wall and refused to eat. Isabel sat by her side and held her hand. The doctor glanced at it as he turned away. It had been so plump and dimpled and white. It was now very thin and white with exposure. It told him far better than complaining how much the poor woman had suffered. He went with a sigh to his patient.

"Stabbed with a bayonet through the shoulder— hard riding from Goliad—no food—no rest—that tells the whole story, doctor."

It was all he could say. A fainting fit followed. Antonia procured some stimulant, and when consciousness returned, assisted her father to dress the wound. Their own coffee was gone, but she begged a cup from someone more fortunate. After the young man had drunk it and had eaten a little bread, he was inclined to make light of his wound and his sufferings.

"Glad to be here at all," he said. "I think I am the only one out of five hundred."

"You cannot mean that you are of Fanning's command?"

"I *was* of Fanning's command. Every man in it has been shot. I escaped by a kind of miracle."

The doctor looked at the Señora. She seemed to be asleep. "Speak low," he said, "but tell me all."

The man sat upon the floor with his back against the wall. The doctor stooped over him. Antonia and Isabel stood beside their father.

"We heard of Urrea's approach at San Patricio. The Irish people of that settlement welcomed Urrea with great rejoicing. He was a Catholic—a defender of the faith. But the American settlers in the surrounding country fled, and Fanning heard that 500 women and children, followed by the enemy, were trying to reach the fortress of Goliad. He ordered Major Ward, with the Georgia battalions, to go and meet the fugitives. Many of the officers entreated him not to divide his men for a report which had come by way of the faithless colony of San Patricio.

"But Fanning thought the risk ought to be taken. He took it, and the 500 women and children proved to be a regiment of Mexican dragoons. They surrounded our infantry on every side, and after two days' desperate fighting, the Georgia battalions were no more. In the meantime, Fanning got the express telling him of the fall of the Alamo and ordering him to unite with General Houston. That might have been a possible thing with 860 men, but it was not possible with 360. However, we made the effort, and on the great prairie we were attacked by the enemy lying in ambush there. Entirely encircled by them, yet still fighting and pressing onward, we defended ourselves until our ammunition gave out.

Then we accepted the terms of capitulation offered by
Urrea, and were marched back to Goliad as prisoners of
war. Santa Anna ordered us all to be shot."

"But you were prisoners of war?"

"Urrea laughed at the articles, and said his only
intention in them was to prevent the loss of Mexican
blood. Most of his officers remonstrated with him, but he
flew into a passion. 'The Señor Presidente's orders are
not to be trifled with. By the Virgin of Guadelupe!' he
cried, 'it would be as much as my own life was worth to
disobey them.'

"It gave the Mexican soldiers pleasure to tell us these
things, and though we scarcely believed such treachery
possible, we were very uneasy. On the eighth day after
the surrender, a Sunday morning, we were marched out
of the fort on pretence of sending us to Louisiana, according to the articles of surrender, and we were in high
spirits at the prospect.

"But I noticed that we were surrounded by a double
row of soldiers, and that made me suspicious. In a few
moments, Fanning was marched into the center and told
to sit down on a low stool. He felt that his hour had
come. He took his watch and his purse and gave them to
some poor woman who stood outside lamenting and
praying for the poor Americans. I shall never forget the
calmness and brightness of his face. The Mexican colonel
raised his sword, the drums beat, and the slaughter
began. Fifty men at a time were shot, and those whom
the guns missed or crippled were dispatched with the
bayonet or lance."

"You escaped. How?"

"When the lips of the officer moved to give the order: Fire! I fell upon my face as if dead. As I lay, I was pierced by a bayonet through the shoulder, but I made no sign of life. After the execution, the camp followers came to rob the dead. A kind-hearted Mexican woman helped me to reach the river. I found a horse tied there, and I took it. I have been on the point of giving up life several times, but I met a man coming here with the news to Houston, and he helped me to hold out."

The doctor was trembling with grief and anger, and he felt Antonia's hand on his shoulder.

"My friend," he whispered, "did you know John Worth?"

"Who did not know him in Fanning's camp? Any of us would have been glad to save poor Jack. He had one friend who refused to live without him."

"Dare Grant?"

"That was the man, young lady. Grant was a doctor, and the Mexicans wanted doctors. They offered him his life for his services, but he would not have it unless his friend's life also was spared. They were shot together. I was watching their faces at the moment. There wasn't a bit of fear in them."

The Señora rose, and came as swiftly as a spirit to them. She looked like a woman walking in her sleep. She touched the stranger. "I heard you. You saw Dare Grant die. But my boy! My boy! Where is my Juan?"

"Maria, darling."

"Don't speak, Roberto. Where is my Juan? Juan Worth?"

"Madam. I am sorry enough, God knows. Juan Worth—was shot."

Then the wretched mother threw up her hands and with an awful cry fell to the ground. It was hours ere she recovered consciousness, and consciousness only restored her to misery.

The distress of the father, the brother, and the sisters of the dead youth was submerged in the speechless despair of the mother. She could not swallow food; she turned away from the sympathy of all who loved her. Even Isabel's caresses were received with an apathy which was terrifying. With the severed curl of her boy's hair in her fingers, she sat in tearless, voiceless anguish.

Poor Antonia, weighed down with the double loss that had come to her, felt, for the first time, as if their condition was utterly hopeless. The mental picture of Juan and Dare meeting their tragic death hand in hand was constantly before her. With all the purity and strength of her heart she loved Dare, but she did not for a moment wish that he had taken a different course. "It is just what I should have expected from him," she said to Isabel. "If he had let poor Jack die alone, I could never have loved him in the same way again. But oh, Isabel, how miserable I am!"

"Sweet Antonia, I can only weep with you. Think of this; it was on last Sunday morning. Do you remember how sad you were?"

"I was in what seemed to be an unreasonable distress. I went away to weep. My very thoughts were tired with their sorrowful journeys up and down my

mind, trying to find out hope and only meeting despair.
Oh, Jack! Dare! what a cruel fate was yours!"

"And mi madre, Antonia? I fear, indeed, that she will
lose her senses. She will not speak to Thomas, nor even
to me. She has not said a prayer since Jack's death. She
cannot sleep. I am afraid of her, Antonia."

"Tonight we are to move further east. Perhaps the
journey may waken her out of this trance of grief. I can
see that our father is wretched about her. And Thomas
wanders in and out of the room as if his heart was
broken."

"Thomas loved Jack. Luis told me that he sat with
him and Lopez, and that he sobbed like a woman. But,
also, he means a great revenge. None of the men slept
last night. They stood by the campfires talking. Sometimes I went to the door and looked out. How awful they
were in the blaze and darkness! I think, indeed, they
could have conquered Santa Anna very easily."

Isabel had not misjudged the spirit of the camp. The
news of the massacre at Goliad was answered by a call
for vengeance that nothing but vengeance could satisfy.
On the following day Houston addressed his little army.
He reminded them that they were the children of the
heroes who fought for liberty at Yorktown, and Saratoga,
and Bunker Hill. He made a soul-stirring review of the
events that had passed; he explained to them their situation, and the designs of the enemy, and how he proposed
to meet them.

His voice, loud as a trumpet with a silver sound,
inspired all who heard it with courage. His large, bright
visage, serious but hopeful, seemed to sun the camp.

"They live too long," he cried, "who outlive freedom. And I promise you that you shall have a full cup of vengeance. For every man that fell fighting at the Alamo, for every one treacherously slaughtered at Goliad, you shall be satisfied. If I seem to be flying before the enemy now, it is for his destruction. Three Mexican armies united, we cannot fight. We can fight them singly. And every mile we make them follow us weakens them, separates them, confuses them. The low lands of the Brazos, the unfordable streams, the morasses, the pathless woods, are in league with us. And we must place our women and children in safety. Even if we have to carry them to General Gaines and the United States troops, we must protect them, first of all. I believe that we shall win our freedom with our own hands; but if the worst come, and we have to fall back to the Sabine, we shall find friends and backers there. I know President Jackson, my old general, the unconquered Christian Mars! Do you think he will desert his countrymen? Never! If we should need help, he has provided it. The freedom of Texas is sure and certain. It is at hand. Prepare to achieve it. We shall take up our march eastward in three hours."

Ringing shouts answered the summons. The camp was in a tumult of preparation immediately. Houston was lending his great physical strength to the mechanical difficulties to be encountered. A crowd of men was around. Suddenly a woman touched him on the arm, and he straightened himself and looked at her.

"You will kill Santa Anna, General? You will kill this fiend?"

"My dear madam—"

He was so moved with pity that he could not for a moment or two give her any stronger assurance. For this suppliant, pallid and frenzied with sorrow, was the once beautiful Señora Worth. He looked at her hollow eyes, and shrunk form, and worn clothing, and remembered with a pang the lovely, gracious lady clad in satin and lace, with a jewelled comb in her fine hair and a jewelled fan in her beautiful hands, and a wave of pity and anger passed like a flame over his face.

"By the memory of my own dear mother, Señora, I will make Santa Anna pay the full price of his cruelties."

"Thank you, Señor," and she glided away with her tearless eyes fixed upon the curl of black hair in her open palm.

chapter 16

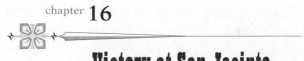

Victory at San Jacinto

The memorial of wrongs, which resulted in the Declaration of Texan Independence, was drawn up with statesmanlike ability by David G. Burnett, a native of New Jersey, a man of great learning, dignity, and experience, who, as early as 1806, sailed from New York to join Miranda in his effort to give Spanish

America liberty. The paper need not be quoted here. It
gave the greatest prominence to the refusal of trial by
jury, the failure to establish a system of public education, the tyranny of military law, the demand that the
colonists should give up arms necessary for their protection or their sustenance, the inciting of the Indians
to massacre the American settlers, and the refusal of the
right to worship the Almighty according to the dictates
of their own consciences. Burnett was elected Governor, and Houston felt that he could now give his whole
attention to military affairs.

   The seat of government was removed to Harrisburg,
a small place on the Buffalo Bayou, and Houston was
sure that this change would cause Santa Anna to di-
verge from his route to Nacogdoches. He dispatched
orders to the men scattered up and down the Brazos
from Washington to Fort Bend—a distance of eighty
miles—to join him on the march to Harrisburg, and he
struck his own camp at the time he had specified.

   In less than twenty-four hours they reached San
Felipe, a distance of twenty-eight miles. The suffering
of the women and children on that march can never be
told. Acts of heroism on the part of the men and of
fortitude on the part of the women that are almost
incredible marked every step of the way. The Señora sat
in her wagon speechless, lost in a maze of melancholy
anguish. She did not seem to heed want, or cold, or
wet, or the utter misery of her surroundings. Her soul
had concentrated all its consciousness upon the strand
of hair she continually smoothed through her fingers.
Dr. Worth, in his capacity of physician, accompanied

the flying families, and he was thus able to pay some
attention to his distraught wife; but she answered
nothing he said to her. If she looked at him, her eyes
either flamed with anger, or expressed something of the
terror to be seen in the eyes of a hunted animal. It was
evident that her childish intelligence had seized upon
him as the most obvious cause of all her loss and misery.

The condition of a wife so beloved almost broke his
heart. The tragic death of his dear son was not so hard
to endure as this living woe at his side. And when they
reached San Felipe and found it in ashes, a bitter cry of
hopeless suffering came from every woman's lips. They
had thought to find there a little food, and a day's
sheltered resting-place. Even Antonia's brave soul
fainted at the want and suffering around her. She had
gold, but it could not buy bread for the little ones,
weeping with hunger and terrified by the fretfulness of
mothers in the last stage of human weariness.

It was on this night Houston wrote: "I will do the
best I can; but be assured the fame of Jackson could
never compensate me for my anxiety and mental pain."
Yet, when he was told that a blind woman and her
seven children had been passed by, and did not know
the enemy were approaching, he delayed the march
until men had been sent back to bring them into safety.

During these days of grief and privation Isabel's
nature grew to its finest proportions. Her patient
efforts to arouse her mother, and her cheerfulness
under the loss of all comforts, were inspiring. Besides
which, she had an inexhaustible fund of sympathy for

the babies. She was never without one in her arms. It was wonderful and pitiful to see the delicately nurtured girl making all kinds of efforts to secure little necessaries for the children she had elected to care for.

At San Felipe they were joined by nearly one hundred men, who also brought word that a fine company was advancing to their aid from Mississippi, and that two large cannon, sent by the people of Cincinnati, were within a few miles. Thus hoping and fearing, hungry and weary to the death, they reached, on the 16th of April, after a march of eighteen miles, a place called McArley's. They had come over a boggy prairie under a cold rain and were depressed beyond expression. But there was a little shelter here for the women and children to sleep under. The men camped in the open. They had not a tent in their possession.

About ten o'clock that night, Doctor Worth was sitting with his wife and Antonia in a corner of a deserted cabin. He had the Señora's wasted hand in his own and was talking to her. She sat in apathetic silence. It was impossible to tell whether she heard or understood him.

"I wonder where Isabel is," said Antonia. With the words the girl entered the room. She had in her arms a little lad of four years old, suffering the tortures of croup.

"Mi madre," she cried, "you know how to save him! He is dying! Save him! Listen to me! The Holy Mother says so." And she laid the child on her knee.

A change like a flash of light passed over the Señora's face. "The poor little one!" Her motherly instincts crushed down everything else. In the child's agony she forgot her own grief. With glad hearts the doctor and Antonia encouraged her in her good work, and when at length the sufferer had been relieved and was sleeping against her breast, the Señora had wept. The stone from her heart had been rolled away by a little child. Her own selfish sorrow had been buried in a wave of unselfish maternal affection. The key to her nature had been found, and henceforward Isabel brought to her every suffering baby.

On the next day they marched ten miles through a heavy rain and arrived at Burnett's settlement. The women had shelter, and the men slept on the wet ground with their arms in their hands. They knew they were in the vicinity of Santa Anna, and all were ready to answer in an instant the three taps of the drum, which was the only instrument of martial music in the camp and was never touched but by Houston.

Another day of eighteen miles brought them to within a short distance of Harrisburg. Santa Anna had just been there, and the place was in ashes. It was evident to all, now, that the day and the hour was at hand. Houston first thought of the 200 families he had in charge, and they were quickly taken over the bayou. When he had seen the last one in this comparative safety, he uttered so fervent a "Thank God!" that the men around unconsciously repeated it. The bayou though narrow was twenty feet deep and full of alligators. There was only one small bridge in the vicinity. He intended its destruction, and thus to make his little band and the deep, dangerous stream a double barrier between the Mexicans and the women and children beyond them. It was after this duty he wrote:

"This morning we are in preparation to meet Santa Anna. We will only be about seven hundred to march, besides the camp guard. But we go to con quest. The troops are in fine spirits, and now is the time for action. I leave the result in the hands of an all-wise God, and I rely confidently in his Provi- dence.

SAM HOUSTON."

The women and children, under a competent guide, continued their march eastward. But they were worn out. Many were unable to put their feet to the ground. The wagons were crowded with these helpless ones. The Señora had so far recovered as to understand that within a few hours Santa Anna and the Americans must meet. And, led by Isabel's passionate hatred, she now showed a vindictiveness beyond that of any other woman.

She spent hours upon her knees, imploring the saints, and the stars, and the angel Michael, to fight against Santa Anna. To Isabel she whispered, "Isabel, do you believe with your heart that Señor Houston and the Americans will be strong enough to kill him?"

"Mi madre, I know it."

"Then do be a little delighted. How can you bear things with such a provoking indifference? But as Luis is safe—"

"Chito! Do not be cruel, mi madre. I could stab Santa Anna with my own hands, when I think of Juan."

No one had before dared to breathe her boy's name in her hearing. She herself had never spoken it. It fell upon the ears of both women like a strain of forgotten music. They looked at each other with eyes full of sweet memory and almost in whispers they began to talk of the dead boy, to recall how lovable, how charming, how affectionate, how obedient he had been. Then the Senora broke open the seals of her sorrow and, with bitter reproaches on herself, confessed that the kiss she had denied her Juan was a load of anguish upon her heart that she could not bear.

"If I had only blessed him," she moaned, "I had saved him from his misfortune. A mother's blessing is such a holy thing! And he knelt at my knees, and begged it. I can see his eyes in the darkness, when my eyes are shut. I can hear his voice when I am asleep. Isabel, I shall never be happy till I see Juan again, and say to him, 'Forgive me, dear one, forgive me.' "

Both were weeping, but Isabel said, bravely: "I am sure that Juan does not blame you now, mi madre. In the other world one understands better. And remember, also, the letter which he wrote you. His last thought was yours. He fell with your name on his lips. These things are certain. And was it not good of Dare to die with him? A friend like that! Out of the talebooks who ever hears of such a thing? Antonia has wept much. In the nights, when she thinks I am asleep, I hear her. Have you seen how thin and white she has grown? I think that my father is very unhappy about her."

"In an hour of mercy may the merciful One remember Dare Grant! I will pray for his peace as long as I live. If he had left Juan—if he had come back alone—I think indeed I should have hated him."

"That was also the opinion of Antonia—she would never have loved him the same. I am sure she would not have married him."

"My good Antonia! Go bring her to me, Isabel. I want to comfort her. She has been so patient with me. I have felt it—felt it every minute. And I have been stupid and selfish and have forgotten that she too was suffering."

The next day it was found impossible to move. The majority of the women had husbands with the army. They had left their wives to secure freedom for their children; but, even if Houston was victorious, they might be wounded and need their help. To be near them in any case was the one thing about which the weary band of women was positive.

"We will not move another inch," said a brave little Massachusetts woman, who had been the natural leader of this domestic Exodus. "We will rest ourselves a little here, and if the Mexicans want some extraordinary fighting they can have it; especially, if they come meddling with us or our children. My husband told me just to get out of reach of shot and shell and wait there till we heard of the victory, and I am for doing *that*, and no other thing."

Nearly two hundred women, bent upon their own way, are not to be taken any other way, and the few old men who had been sent to guide the party and shoot what game was necessary for their support surrendered at once to this feminine mutiny. Besides, the condition of the boys and girls between seven and fourteen was really a deplorable one. They were too old to be cared for as infants, and they had been obliged, with the strength of children, to accomplish the labor of men and women. Many were crippled in their feet; others were continually on the point of swooning.

It was now the 20th of April. The Senora and her daughters had been six weeks with the American army, exposed to all the privations which such a life entailed. But the most obvious of these privations were, perhaps, those which were most easily borne. Women endure great calamities better than the little annoyances affecting those wants which are part and parcel of their sex or their caste. It was not the necessaries so much as the luxuries of life which the Senora missed—the changes of raiment—the privacy—the quiet—the regularity of events.

During the whole of the 20th, there was almost a Sabbath stillness. It was a warm, balmy day. The wearied children were under the wagons and under the trees, sleeping the dead sleep of extreme exhaustion. The mothers, wherever it was possible, slept also. The guides were a little apart, listening and smoking. If they spoke, it was only in monosyllables. Rest was so much more needed than food that little or no attempt was made to cook until near sundown.

At dawn next morning—nay, a little before dawn—when all was chill, and gray, and misty, and there was not a sound but the wailing of a sick child, the Señora touched her daughters. Her voice was strange to them; her face solemnly happy.

"Antonia! Isabel! I have seen Juan! My eyes were shut, but I have seen him. He was a beautiful shadow, with a great, shadowy host around him. And he bent on me such eyes! Now I am happy. I will weep no more. They put my Juan's body in the grave, but they have not buried *him*."

All day she was silent and full of thought, but her face was smiling and hopeful, and she had the air of one waiting for some assured happiness. About three o'clock in the afternoon she stood up quickly and cried, "Hark! the battle has begun!" Everyone listened intently, and after a short pause the oldest of the guides nodded. "I'd give the rest of my life to be young again," he said, "just for three hours to be young, and behind Houston!"

About ten o'clock in the morning of the 22nd, a horseman was seen coming toward the camp at full speed. Women and children stood breathlessly waiting his approach. No one could speak. If a child moved, the movement was angrily reproved. The tension was too great to admit of a touch through any sense. Some, unable to bear the extended strain, sank upon the ground and covered their faces with their hands. But the half-grown children, wan with privations and fever, ragged and barefoot, watched steadily the horse and its rider, their round, gleaming eyes full of wonder and fear.

"It is Thomas," said the Señora.

As he came near, and the beat of the horse's hoofs could be heard, a cry almost inarticulate, shrill and agonizing in its intensity, broke simultaneously from the anxious women. It was one cry from many hearts, all at the last point of endurance. Thomas Worth understood it. He flung his hat up, and answered with a joyful "Hurrah!"

When he reached the camp, every face was wet with tears, and a crowd of faces was instantly round him. All the agonies of war were on them. He raised himself in his stirrups and shouted out:

"You may all go back to your homes! Santa Anna is completely overthrown! The Mexican army is destroyed! There will be no more fighting, no more fears. The independence of Texas is won! No matter where you come from, YOU ARE ALL TEXANS NOW! Victory! Freedom! Peace! My dear friends, go back to your homes. Your husbands will join you at the San Jacinto."

Then he dismounted and sought his mother and sisters. With joyful amazement he recognized the change in the Señora. "You look like yourself, dear mother," he said. "Father sends you this kiss. He would have brought it, but there are a few wounded men to look after, and also I can ride quicker. Antonia, cheer up my dear!—and Isabel, little darling, you will not need to cry anymore for your ribbons, and mantillas, and pretty dresses."

"Thomas! You have not much feeling, I think. What I want to know about is Luis. You think of no one; and as for my dresses and mantillas, I dare say Fray Ignatius has sold or burned them."

"Queridita! Was I cruel? Luis is well. He has not a scratch. He was in the front of the battle, too."

"That, of course. Would you imagine that Luis would be at the rear? He is General Houston's friend, and one lion knows another lion."

"Pretty one, do not be angry with me. I will tell you some good news. Luis is coming here, unless you go back at once with me."

"We will go back with you, Thomas. I am full of impatience. I remember my dear home. I will go to it, like a bird to its nest."

In half an hour they had turned the heads of their horses westward again. They went so rapidly, and were under so much excitement, that sustained conversation was impossible. The Señora fell into a sound sleep as soon as the first homeward steps had been taken and slept till they reached the victorious camp and her husband awakened her with a kiss.

How different was the return to the ground west of the Buffalo Bayou! The very atmosphere was changed. A day or two of spring had brought out the flowers and unfolded every green thing. Doctor Worth took his family to a fine Mexican marquee,[49] and among other comforts the Señora found there the chocolate she had so long craved.

In a short time a luxurious meal was prepared by Antonia, and just as they were sitting down to it, Luis and Lopez entered the tent together. Isabel had expected the visit and prepared for it as far as her limited wardrobe permitted. Her fine hair, her bright eyes, her perfect face and form, and the charming innocence of

---

[49]marquee—tent

her manners, adorned her as the color and perfume of the rose make the beauty of the flower. She was so lovely that she could dare to banter Luis on the splendor of his attire.

"It is evident, mi madre, that Luis has found at least the baggage of a major-general. Such velvet and silver embroidery! Such a silk sash! They are fit at the very least for a sultan of the Turks."

A wonderful exaltation possessed both Luis and Lopez. The sombre, handsome face of the latter was transfigured by it. He kissed the hand of the Señora, and then turned to Antonia. Her pallor and emaciation shocked him. He could only murmur, "Señorita!" But she saw the surprise, the sorrow, the sympathy, yes, the adoring love in his heart, and she was thankful to him for the reticence that relieved her from special attention.

As yet the ladies had not spoken of the battle. It was won. That great fact had been as much as they could bear at first. The Señora wanted to sleep. Isabel wanted to see Luis. Only Antonia was anxious for the details, and she had been busy in preparing the respectable meal which her mother had so long craved. The apparent indifference was natural enough. The assurance of good fortune is always sufficient for the first stage of relief from anxiety. When the most urgent personal feelings have been satisfied, then comes the demand for detail and discussion. So now, as they sat together, the Señora said:

"No one has told me anything about the battle. Were you present, Roberto?"

"I had that great honor, Maria. Lopez and Luis were with the cavalry, and Ortiz also has had some satisfaction for all his wrongs."

"Very good! But I am impatient for the story; so are Antonia and—bah! Isabel is listening to another story. One must excuse her. We expected the battle on the twentieth, but no!"

"The enemy were expecting it also, and were in high spirits and perfect preparation. Houston thought it prudent to dash their enthusiasm by uncertainty and waiting. But at dawn, on the twenty-first, we heard the three taps of the drum, and seven hundred soldiers sprang to their feet as one man. Houston had been watching all night. He spoke to us with a tongue of fire and then, while we cooked and ate our breakfast, he lay down and slept. The sun came up without a cloud, and shone brightly on his face. He sprang to his feet and said to Burleson, as he saluted him: 'The sun of Austerlitz[50] has risen again.'

"Some one brought him a piece of cornbread and broiled beef. He sat upon the grass and ate it. For many weeks I had not seen his countenance so bright; all traces of trouble and anxiety were gone. He called Deaf Smith—the scout of scouts—and quickly ordered him to cut down the only bridge across the bayou.

"At nine o'clock, General Cos joined Santa Anna with five thousand four hundred and forty men, and for a moment I thought we had made a mistake in not attack-

---

[50]Austerlitz—a town in Czechoslovakia where Napoleon defeated the Russian and Austrian armies in 1805

ing the enemy before his reinforcements came up. But the knowledge that Cos was present raised enthusiasm to the highest pitch. Our troops remembered his parole at the Alamo, and the shameful manner in which he had broken it; there was not a man present who did not long to kill him for it.

"About three o'clock in the afternoon, Houston ordered the attack. The seven hundred Americans were divided into three bodies. I saw Houston in the very center of the line, and I have a confused memory of Milard and Lamar, Burleson and Sherman and Wharton, in front of their divisions."

"Were the Mexicans expecting the attack, Father?"

"They were in perfect order, Antonia. And when Sherman shouted the battle-cry: 'REMEMBER THE ALAMO! GOLIAD AND THE ALAMO!' it was taken up by the whole seven hundred, and such a shout of vengeance mortal ears never heard before. The air was full of it, and it appeared to be echoed and repeated by innumerable voices.

Lopez rose at the words. It was impossible for him to express himself sufficiently in an attitude of repose. His eyes glowed like fire, his dark face was like a flame, he threw up his hands as he cried:

"Nothing comparable to that charge was ever made on earth! If I had seen through the smoke and vapor the mighty shade of Bowie leading it, I should not have been surprised."

"And you are not alone in the thought, Lopez. I heard General Sherman say, 'Poor Fanning! He has been blamed for not obeying Houston's orders. I think he

obeyed them today.' At the moment I did not comprehend; but now it is plain to me. He thought Fanning
had been present, and perhaps it was this belief made
him so impetuous and invincible. He fought like one
who had forgot that he was flesh and blood."

"But then, Roberto, nothing shall persuade me that
my countrymen are cowards."

"On the contrary, Maria, they kept their ground
with great courage. They were slain by hundreds just
where they stood when the battle began. Twenty-six
officers and nearly seven hundred men were left dead
upon the field. But the flight was still more terrible.
Into the bayou horses and men rolled down together.
The deep black stream became red; it was choked up
with their dead bodies, while the mire and water of the
morass was literally bridged with the smothered mules
and horses and soldiers."

"The battle began at three o'clock; but we heard the
firing only for a very short time," said Antonia.

"After we reached their breastworks it lasted just
eighteen minutes. By four, the whole Mexican army
was dead, or flying in every direction, and the pursuit
and slaughter continued until twilight. Truly an unseen
power made all our moves for us. It was a military
miracle, for our loss was only eight killed and seventeen
wounded."

"I am sorry Houston is among the wounded."

"His ankle-bone is shattered. He is suffering much.
I was with him when he left the field and I marveled at
his patience and dignity. The men crowded around
him. They seized his bridle; they clasped his hands.

'Have we done well today, General? Are you satisfied with us?' they cried.

" 'You have covered yourselves with glory,' he answered. 'You have written a grand page in American history this day, boys. For it was not for fame nor for empire you fought, but for your rights as freemen, for your homes and your faith.'

"The next moment he fell from his horse, and we laid him down at the foot of an oak tree. He had fainted from loss of blood and the agony of his wound, combined with the superhuman exertions and anxieties of the past week."

"But he is better now?"

"Yes. I dressed the wound as well as my appliances permitted, but he will not be able to use his foot for some time. No one slept that night. Weary as the men were, their excitement and happiness were too great for the bonds of sleep. In the morning the rich spoils of the enemy's camp were divided among them. Houston refused any part in them. 'My share of the honor is sufficient,' he said. Yet the spoils were very valuable ones to men who but a few hours before had nothing but the clothing they wore and the arms they carried. Among them were nearly one thousand stand of English muskets, three hundred valuable mules, one hundred fine horses, provisions, clothing, tents, and at least twelve thousand dollars in silver."

At this moment Thomas Worth entered the marquee, and, in an excited manner, said:

"Santa Anna is taken! Santa Anna is taken!"

"Taken!" cried the Señora in a passion. "Is it possible the wretch is yet in this world? I was assuring myself that he was in one not so comfortable. Why is he not killed? It is an inconceivable insult to humanity to let him live. Have you thought of your brother Juan? Give me the knife in your belt, Thomas, if you cannot use it."

"Maria, my life!" interjected the doctor. "Thomas could not wisely kill so important a prisoner. Texas wants him to secure her peace and independence. The lives of all the Americans in Mexico may depend upon his. Mere personal vengeance on him would be too dear a satisfaction. On the battlefield he might have been lawfully slain—and he was well looked for—but now, no."

"Might have been slain! He ought to have been slain a thousand times over."

The doctor turned to his son. "Thomas, tell us about the capture."

"I was riding with a young lieutenant, called Sylvester, from Cincinnati, and he saw a man hiding in the grass. He was in coarsest clothing, but Sylvester noticed under it linen of fine cambric. He said: 'You are an officer, I perceive, sir.' The man denied it, but when he could not escape, he asked to be taken to General Houston. Sylvester tied him to his bridle-rein, and we soon learned the truth; for as we passed the Mexican prisoners, they lifted their hats and said, with a murmur of amazement, 'El Presidente!'

"The news spread like wildfire. As we took him through the camp he trembled at the looks and words that assailed him, and prayed us continually not to let him be slain. We took him to Houston in safety. Houston was resting on the ground, having had, as my father knows, a night of great suffering. Santa Anna approached him, and, laying his hand on his heart, said: 'I am General Antonio Lopez de Santa Anna, President of the Mexican Republic, and I claim to be your prisoner of war.' Houston pointed to a seat, and then sent for Santa Anna's secretary, Almonte, who is also a prisoner, and who speaks English perfectly.'

"When Almonte came, he embraced Santa Anna, and addressing Houston, said: 'General, you are born to a great destiny. You have conquered the Napoleon of the West. Generosity becomes the brave and the fortunate.'

"Houston answered, sternly: 'You should have remembered that sentiment at the Alamo and at Goliad.'

The discussion upon this event lasted until midnight. But the ladies retired to their own tent much earlier. They knelt together in grateful prayer, and then kissed each other upon their knees. It was so sweet to lie down once more in safety—to have the luxury of a tent, and a mattress, and pillow.

"Blessed be the hand of God! my children," said the Señora. "And may the angels give us in our dreams grateful thoughts."

In the dark, Isabel whispered: "Forgive me for being happy, sweet Antonia. Indeed, when I smiled on Luis, I was often thinking of you. In my joy, I do not forget that one great awful grave at Goliad. But a woman must hide so many things; do you comprehend me, Antonia?"

"Queridita," she whispered, "I comprehend all. God has done right. If He had said to me, 'One must be taken and the other left,' I should have prayed, 'Spare then my little sister all sorrow.' Good-night, Iza darling."

At the same moment, the white curtains of the marquee, in which the doctor sat talking with his son and Luis and Lopez, were opened, and the face of Ortiz showed brown and glowing between them.

"Señors," he said, as he advanced to them, "I am satisfied. I have been appointed on the guard over Santa Anna. He has recognized me. He has to obey my orders. Will you think of that?" Then taking the doctor's hand he raised it to his lips. "Señor, I owe this satisfaction to you. You have made me my triumph. How shall I repay you?"

"By being merciful in the day of your power, Ortiz."

"I assure you that I am not so presumptuous, Señor. Mercy is the right of the Divinity. It is beyond my capacity. Besides which, it is not likely the Divinity will trouble himself about Santa Anna. I have, therefore, to obey the orders of the great, the illustrious Houston, which are to prevent his escape at all risks. May St. James give me the opportunity, Señors! In this happy hour, adios!"

Then Lopez bent forward, and with a smile touched the doctor's hand. "Will you now remember the words I said of Houston? Did I not tell you, that success was with him? that on his brow was the line of fortune? that he was the loadstone in the breast of freedom?"

chapter **17**

Home Again

*T*he vicinity of a great battlefield is a dreadful
place after the lapse of a day or two. The bayou
and the morass had provided sepulcher for hundreds of
slain Mexicans, but hundreds still lay upon the open
prairie. Over it, birds of prey hung in dark clouds,
heavy-winged, sombre, and silent. Nothing disturbed
them. They took no heed of the living. And yet, though
innocent as the elements, they were odious in the sight
of all.

Before daylight in the morning the Señora and her
daughters were ready to begin their homeward journey.
The doctor could not accompany them; General Houston and the wounded Americans being dependent
largely upon his care and skill. But Luis Alveda and
Lopez Navarro received an unlimited furlough, and
about a dozen Mexican prisoners of war belonging to
San Antonio were released on Navarro's assurance and
were permitted to travel with the party as camp servants. It was likely, also, that they would be joined by a
great many of the families who had accompanied the
great flight, for on the preceding evening Houston had
addressed the army and told the householders and
farmers to go home and plant their corn.

Full of happiness, the ladies prepared for their journey. A good army wagon drawn by eight mules, and
another wagon containing two tents and everything
necessary for a comfortable journey, was waiting for
them. The doctor bid them good-by with smiles and
cheerful promises. They were going home. The war was
over. Independence was won. They had the hope of
permanent peace. The weather also was as the weather
might have been among the fields of Eden. The heavens
were cloudless, the air sweet and fresh, and the wild
honeysuckles, with their spread hands full of scent,
perfumed the prairies mile after mile.

Even Lopez was radiantly happy. Most unusual
smiles lighted up his handsome face, and he jingled the
silver ornaments on his bridle pleasantly as he cantered
sometimes a little in advance of the wagon, sometimes in
the rear, occasionally by its side. Now and then he would
bend forward to lift his hat to the ladies and inquire after
their comfort, and smiles would be exchanged.

Luis kept close to Isabel, and her lovely face and
merry chatter beguiled him from all other observations.
A little before noon they halted in a beautiful wood; a
tent was spread for the ladies, the animals were loosened
from their harness, and a luxurious meal was laid upon
the grass. Then the siesta was taken, and at three o'clock
travel was resumed until near sunset, when the camp
was made for the night. The same order was followed
every day, and the journey was in every sense an easy and
delightful one.

On the third afternoon, the Señora and Isabel were
taking a siesta, but Antonia could not sleep. After one or

two efforts she was thoroughly aroused by the sound of voices which had been very familiar to her in the black days of the flight—those of a woman and her seven children. Antonia had helped her in many ways, and she still felt an interest in the family's welfare. It appeared now to be assured. Antonia found her camping in a little grove of mulberry trees. She had recovered her health; her children were noisy and happy, and her husband, a tall, athletic man, with a determined eye and very courteous manners, was unharnessing the mules from a fine Mexican wagon, part of the lawful spoils of war. They, too, were going home—"back to the Brazos," said the woman affectionately. "And we're in a considerable hurry," she added, "because it's about time to get the corn in. Jake lays out to plant fifty acres this year."

They talked a short time together, and then Antonia walked slowly into the deeper shadows of the wood. She found a wide rock and she sat down in the sweet gloom to think of the beloved dead. She had often longed for some quiet spot where, alone with God and nature, she could, just for once, give to her sorrow a free expression.

Now the opportunity seemed to be hers. She began to recall her whole acquaintance with Dare—their hours of pleasant study—their sails upon the river—their talks by the fireside—the happy Sundays, when they walked in the house of God together. She recalled also the time of hope and anxiety after the storming of the Alamo, and then the last heroic act of his life. She thought of the loving brother who perished at his side and of the joy he had brought to their home.

In the drift of such thoughts, she found herself
smiling through happy tears. Antonia had not anticipated the holy peace which forbid her sorrow as 'those
which have no hope.' Suddenly she understood the
words of the psalmist David: "Yea, though I walk
through the valley of the shadow of death, I will fear no
evil: for thou art with me; thy rod and thy staff they
comfort me."

At length, she rose to return to the camp. A few
yards nearer to it she saw Lopez sitting in a reverie as
profound as her own had been. He stood up to meet
her. The patience, the pathos, the exaltation in her face
touched his heart as no words could have done. He
said, only: "Senorita, if I knew how to comfort you!"

"I have a Divine Comforter, Señor. He gives me
peace."

Lopez smiled and looked heavenward. "I am sure
that I shall never know two souls more pure, more
faithful, more brave. Juan was as a brother to me, and
I count it among God's blessings to have known a man
like Señor Grant."

Antonia looked at him gratefully. Tears uncalled-for
sprang into the eyes of both; they clasped hands and
walked mutely back to the camp together. For the
sentiment which attends the realization that all is over
is gathered silently into the heart; it is too deep for
words.

They found the camp already in that flurry of
excitement always attendant upon its rest and rising,
and the Señora was impatiently inquiring for her eldest
daughter.

"Gracious Maria! Is that you, Antonia? At this hour
we are all your servants, I think. I, at least, have been
waiting upon your pleasure." Then, perceiving the
traces of sorrow and emotion on her face, she added,
with an unreasonable querulousness: "I bless God
when I see how He has provided for women; giving
them tears, when they have no other employment for
their time."

"Mi madre, I am sorry to have kept you waiting. I
hope that you have forgotten nothing. Where is your
mantilla? Is there water in the wagon?"

"Nothing has been provided. Things most necessary
are forgotten, no doubt. When you neglect such matters, what less could happen?"

But such little breezes of temper were soon over.
The influences surrounding, the prospects in advance,
were too exhilarating to permit of anything but passing
shadows, and after an easy, delightful journey, they
reached at length the charming vicinity of the romantic
city of the sword. They had but another five miles ride,
and it was the Señora's pleasure to take it at the hour of
midnight. She did not wish her return to be observed
and talked about; she was in reality very much mortified by the condition of her own and her daughters'
wardrobes.

Consequently, though they made their noon camp so
near to their journey's end, they rested there until San
Antonio was asleep and dreaming. It was the happiest
rest of all the delightful ones they had known. The
knowledge that it was the last stage of a journey so
remarkable, made everyone attach a certain tender

value to the hours never to come back, to the experiences never to be repeated.

The Señora was gay as a child, and Isabel shared and accentuated her enthusiasms. Luis was expressing his happiness in a variety of songs; now glorifying his love in some pretty romance or serenade, again assuring liberty, or Texas, that he would be delighted at any moment to lay down his life for their sakes. Antonia was quite as much excited in her own way, which was naturally a much quieter way, and Lopez sat under a great pecan-tree, casting admiring glances at everyone.

As the sun set, the full moon rose as it rises nowhere but over Texan or Asian plains; golden and glorious, seeming to fill the whole heaven and the whole earth with a soft, exquisite glow. The commonest thing under it was transfigured into something lovely and fairylike, and the dullest souls swelled and rose like the tides under its influence.

Antonia took from their stores the best they had, and a luxurious supper was spread upon the grass. The meal might have been one of ten courses, it occupied so long. It provoked such mirth, such a rippling stream of reminiscence, and finally, a sweetly solemn retrospect of the sorrows and mercies and triumphs of the campaign they had shared together. This latter feeling soon dominated all others.

The delicious light, the sensuous atmosphere, the white turrets and towers of the city shining on the horizon like some mystical vision of heaven were all elements conducive to a grave yet happy seriousness.

No one intended to sleep. They were to rest in the moonlight until the hour of eleven, and then make their last stage. This night they instinctively kept close together. The Señora had mentally reached that point where it was not unpleasant to talk over troubles, and to amplify especially her own share of them.

A slight disappointment, however, awaited the Señora. Without asking any questions, without taking anything into consideration, perhaps because she feared to ask or consider, she had assumed that she would immediately reenter her own home. With the unreason of a child, she had insisted upon expecting that somehow, or by some not explained efforts, she would find her house precisely as she had left it. Little had been said of its occupancy by Fray Ignatius and his brothers. Perhaps she did not quite believe in the statement; perhaps she expected Fray Ignatius to respect the arrangements which he knew had been so dear to her.

It was therefore a trial—indeed, something of a shock—when she found they were to be the guests of Navarro, and when it was made clear to her that her own home had been dismantled and rearranged and was still in the possession of the Church. But, with a child's unreason, she had also a sweet ductility of nature; she was easily persuaded, easily pleased, and quite ready to console herself with the assurance that it only needed Doctor Worth's presence and personal influence to drive away all intruders upon her rights.

In the mean time she was contented. The finest goods in San Antonio were sent early on the following morning to her room, and the selection of three entire

wardrobes gave her abundance of delightful employment. She almost wept with joy as she passed the fine
lawns and rich silks through her worn fingers. And
when she could cast off forever her garment of weari-
ful wanderings and array herself in the splendid robes
which she wore with such grace and pleasure, she was
an honestly grateful woman.

Then she permitted Lopez to let her old acquaintances know of her presence in her native city, and she
was comforted when she began to receive calls from
the Señora Alveda, and Judge and Señora Valdez, and
many other of her friends and associates. They encouraged her to talk of her sufferings and her great
loss. Even the judge thought it worth his while, now,
to conciliate the simple little woman. He had wisdom
enough to perceive that Mexican domination was over
and that the American influence of Doctor Worth was
likely to be of service to him.

The Señora found herself a heroine; more than
that, she became aware that for some reason those
who had once patronized her were now disposed to
pay her a kind of court. But this did not lessen her
satisfaction; she suspected no motive but real kindness, for she had that innate rectitude which has
always confidence in the honesty of others.

There was now full reconciliation between Luis
and his mother and uncles, and his betrothal to Isabel
was acknowledged with all the customary rejoicings
and complimentary calls and receptions. Life quickly
began to fall back into its well-defined grooves; if
there was anything unusual, everyone made an effort

to pass it by without notice. The city was conspicu-
ously in this mind. American rule was accepted in the
quiescent temper with which men and women accept
weather which may or may not be agreeable, but which
is known to be unavoidable. Americans were coming
by hundreds and by thousands. Those Mexicans who
could not make up their minds to become Texans and
to assimilate with the new elements sure to predomi-
nate were quietly breaking up their homes and transfer-
ring their interests across the Rio Grande.

They were not missed, even for a day. Some American was ready to step into their place, and the pushing,
progressive spirit of the race was soon evident in the
hearty way with which they set to work, not only to
repair what war had destroyed but to inaugurate those
movements which are always among their first necessities. Ministers, physicians, teachers, mechanics of all
kinds, were soon at work; churches were built, Bibles
were publicly sold, or given away; schools were adver-
tised; the city was changing its tone as easily as a
woman changes the fashion of her dress. The ensign of
the young Republic soon floated above the twice glorious Alamo: a bright blue standard, with one white star
in the center. The lonely star in its field of blue touched
every heart's chivalry. It said to them, "I stand alone! I
have no sister states to encourage and help me! I rely
only on the brave hearts and strong arms that I set me
here!"

A short time after their return, the Señora had a
letter from her husband, saying that he was going to
New Orleans with General Houston, whose wound was

in a dangerous condition. Thomas Worth had been
appointed to an important post in the civil government,
and his labors, like those of all the public men of Texas
at that date, were continuous and Herculean. It was
impossible for the doctor to leave them at that time, but
he assured his wife that he would return as soon as he
had placed Houston in the hands of skillful surgeons.
He asked her, until then, to be as happy as her circumstances permitted.

She was quite willing to obey the request. The
Señora found many sources of content and pleasure,
until the early days of June brought back to her the
husband she so truly loved and with him the promise of
a return to her own home. Indeed the difficulties in the
way of this return vanished before they were met. Fray
Ignatius concluded that his short lease had fully ex-
pired, and when Dr. Worth went armed with the legal
process necessary to resume his rights, he found his
enemy had already surrendered them. The house was
empty. Nothing of its old splendor remained. Every one
of its properties had been scattered. The poor Señora
walked through the desolate rooms with a heartache.

"It was precisely in this spot that the sideboard
stood, Roberto!—the sideboard that my cousin Johar
presented to me. It came from the City of Mexico, and
there was not another like it. I shall regret it all my
life."

"Maria, dearest, it might have been worse. The
silver which adorned it is safe. And I bought you a far
more beautiful sideboard in New Orleans—the very
newest style, Maria."

"Roberto! Roberto! How happy you make me! To be sure my cousin Johar's sideboard was already shabby— and to have a sideboard from New Orleans, that, indeed, is something to talk about!"

"Besides, which, dearest one, I bought new furniture for the parlors, and for your own apartments; also for Antonia's and Isabel's rooms. Indeed, Maria, I thought it best to provide afresh for the whole house."

"How wonderful! No wife in San Antonio has a husband so good. I will never condescend to speak of you when other women talk of their husbands. New furniture for my whole house! But when, Roberto, will these things arrive? Is there danger on the road they are coming? Might not someone take them away? I shall not be able to sleep until I am sure they are safe."

"I chartered a schooner in New Orleans, and came with them to the Bay of Espiritu Santo. There I saw them placed upon wagons, and only left them after the customs had been paid in the interior—sixty miles away. You may hire servants at once to prepare the rooms: the furniture will be here in about three days."

"I am the happiest woman in the world, Roberto!" And she really felt herself to be so. Thoughtful love could have devised nothing more likely to bridge pleasantly and surely over the transition between the past and the coming life. Every fresh piece of furniture unpacked was a new wonder and a new delight. With her satin skirts tucked daintily clear of soil, and her mantilla wrapped around her head and shoulders, she went from room to room, interesting herself in every strip of carpet, and every yard of drapery. Her delight was infectious. The

doctor smiled to find himself comparing shades, and
gravely considering the arrangement of chairs and
tables.

But how was it possible for so loving a husband and
father to avoid sharing the pleasure he had provided?
Isabel was even more excited than her mother. All this
grandeur had a double meaning to her; it would reflect
honor upon the betrothal receptions which would be
given for Luis and herself—"amber satin and white lace
is exactly what I should have desired, Antonia," she said
delightedly. "How exceedingly suitable it will be to me!
And those delicious chintzes and dimities for our bed-
rooms! Did you ever conceive of things so beautiful?"

Antonia was quite ready to echo her delight. Housekeeping and homemaking, in all its ways, was her
lovable talent. It was really Antonia who saw all the
plans and the desires of the Señora thoroughly carried
out. It was her clever fingers and natural taste which
gave to every room that air of comfort and refinement
which all felt and admired.

On the fourth of July the doctor and his family ate
together their first dinner in their renovated home. The
day was one that he never forgot, and he was glad to
link it with a domestic occurrence so happy and so
fortunate.

"My wife and daughters, I believe I shall live to see
the lone star set among her sister stars! I shall live to
say, I dwell in San Antonio, which is the loveliest city in
the loveliest state of the American Union. For I was
born an American citizen, and I ask this favor of God,
that I may also die an American citizen."

"Mi Roberto, when you die I shall not long survive you. And now that the house is made so beautiful with so much new furniture—how can you speak of dying?"

"And why, father, speak of the American Union when you have fought so hard for the independence of Texas?"

"Because, Antonia, I would have Texas go free into a union of free states. This was the hope of Houston. 'We can have help,' he often said to his little army, 'a word will call help from Nacogdoches,—but we will emancipate ourselves. If we go into the American States, we will go as equals; we will go as men who have won the right to say: Let us dwell under the same flag, for we are brothers!' "

chapter **18**

Under One Flag

As the years go on they bring many changes— changes that come as naturally as the seasons and scarcely startle the subjects of them, till time discloses their vitality and extent. Between the ages of twenty and thirty, ten years do not seem very destructive to life. The woman at eighteen, and twenty-eight, if changed, is usually ripened and improved; the man at thirty, finer and more mature than he was at twenty. But

when this same period is placed to women and men who
are either approaching fifty, or have passed it, the
change is distinctly felt.

It was even confessed by the Señora one morning in
the beginning of March, though the sun was shining
warmly, and the flowers blooming, and the birds singing
as though it was the first season of creation.

"I am far from being as gay and strong as I wish to
be, Roberto," she said. "And today, consider what a
company there is coming! If General Houston is to be
added to it, I shall be as weary as I shall be happy."

"He is the simplest of men; a cup of coffee, a bit of
steak—"

"How you talk! But is it possible to receive him like
a common mortal? He is a hero—"

"Well, then, you have servants, Maria, dear."

"Servants! Bah! Of what use are they, Roberto,
since they also have got hold of American ideas?"

"Isabel and Antonia will be here."

"Let me only enumerate to you, Roberto. Thomas
and his wife and four children arrived last night. You
may at this moment hear the little Maria crying. I dare
say Pepita is washing the child and using soap which is
very disagreeable. I have always admired the wife of
Thomas, but I think she is too fond of her own way with
the children. I give her advices which she does not
take."

"They are her own children, dearest."

"They are also my own grandchildren."

"Well, well, we must remember that Abbie is a little
Puritan. She believes in bringing up children strictly,

and it is good, for Thomas would spoil them. As for
Isabel's boys—"

"God be blessed! Isabel's boys are entirely charming. They have been corrected at my own knee. There
are not more beautifully behaved boys in the christened
world."

"And Antonia's little Christina?"

"She is already an angel. Roberto, when I rise I am
very stiff: I think, indeed, I have some rheumatism."

"That is not unlikely—and also Maria, you have now
some years."

"Let that be confessed; but the good God knows that
I lost all my youth in that awful flight of 'thirty-six."

"Maria, we all left or lost something on that dark
journey. Today, we shall recover its full value."

"To be sure—that is what is said—we shall see. Will
you now send Dolores to me? Tell me, Roberto, what
dress is your preference; it is your eyes, beloved, I wish
to please."

Robert Worth was not too old to feel charmed and
touched by the compliment. And he was not a thought-
less or churlish husband; he knew how to repay such a
wifely compliment, and it was a pleasant sight to see
the aged companions standing hand in hand before the
handsome suits which Dolores had spread out for her
mistress to examine.

He looked at the purple and the black and the white
robes, and then he looked at the face beside him. It
was faded, and had lost its oval shape, but its coloring
was yet beautiful and the large, dark eyes tender and
bright below the snow-white hair. After a few minutes'

consideration, he touched, gently, a robe of white satin. "Put this on, Maria," he said, "and your white mantilla, and your best jewels. The occasion will excuse the utmost splendor."

The choice delighted her. She had really wished to wear it, and someone's judgment to endorse her own inclinations was all that was necessary to confirm her wish. Dolores found her in the most delightful temper. She sat before the glass, smiling and talking, while her maid piled high the snowy plaits and curls and crowned them with the jewelled comb, only worn on very great festivals. Her form was still good, and the white satin fell gracefully from her throat to her small feet. There was the flash of diamonds, and the moonlight glimmer of pearls beneath graceful, veiling folds of her mantilla, and at her belt a few white lilies. She was exceedingly pleased with her own appearance, and her satisfaction gave an ease and a sense of authority to her air and movements which was charming.

"By Maria's grace, I am a very pretty old lady," she said to herself, "and I think I shall astonish my daughter-in-law a little. One is afraid of these calm, cool, northern women, but I feel today that even Abbie must be proud of me."

Indeed, her entrance into the large parlor made quite a sensation. She could see the quiet pleasure in her husband's face, and her son Thomas, after one glance, put down the child on his knee and went to meet her. "Mi madre," he whispered with a kiss. He had not used the pretty Spanish word for years, but in the sudden rush of admiring tenderness, his boyish heart came back to him, and quite unconsciously he used his boyhood's speech. After this, she was not the least in awe of her wise daughter-in-law. She touched her cheek kindly, and asked her about the children, and was immeasurably delighted when Abbie said: "How beautiful you are today! I wish I had your likeness to send to Boston. Robert, come here and look at your grandmother! I want you to remember, as long as you live, how grandmother looks today." Robert—a fine lad eight years old, accustomed to implicit obedience—put down the book he was reading, planted himself squarely before the Señora, and looked at her attentively, as if she was a lesson to be learned.

"Well then, Roberto?"

"I am glad I have such a pretty grandmother. Will you let me kiss you?" and the cool, calm northern woman's eyes filled with tears, as she brought her younger children, one by one, for the Señora's caress. As the doctor and his son watched this pretty domestic drama with hearts full of pride and happiness, the door was flung open with a vigor which made everyone turn to it with expectation. A splendid little lad sprang in, and without any consideration for satin and lace, clung to the Senora. He was her image—a true Yturbide, young as he was—beautiful and haughty as his Castilian ancestors.

Isabel and Luis followed. Isabel was more lovely than ever, richly dressed in American fashion, full of pretty enthusiasms, vivacious, charming, and quite at her ease. She had been married eight years. She was a fashionable woman, and an authority upon all social subjects.

Luis also was wonderfully improved. The light-hearted gaiety, which ten years ago had bubbled over in continual song, was still there, but it was under control, evident only because it made perpetual sunshine on his face. He had taken the doctor's advice—completed his study of English and Mexican law—and become a famous referee in cases of disputed Mexican claims and title deeds. His elegant form and handsome, olive face looked less picturesque in the dull, uncompromising stiffness of broadcloth. But it gained by the change a certain air of reliability and importance, an air not to be dispensed with in a young lawyer already aspiring to a seat among the lawmakers of his State.

"We called upon Antonia," said Isabel, "as we came here. Of course she was engaged with Lopez. They were reading a book together, and even on such a day as this were taking, with the most blessed indifference, a minute at a time. They will join us on the Plaza. I represented to them that they might miss a good position. 'That has been already secured,' said Lopez, with that exasperating repose which only the saints could endure with patience. For that reason, I consider Antonia a saint to permit it. As for me, I should say: 'The house is on fire, Lopez! Will it please you for once to feel a little excited?'"

"Here are the carriages," cried Thomas Worth.

"Your mother and I will go first, Thomas, and we will take Abbie and your eldest son. I shall see you in your place. Luis, bring your boy with you; he has intelligence and will remember the man he will see today, and may never see again."

On the Plaza, close to the gates of the Alamo, a rostrum had been erected, and around it were a few stands set apart for the carriages of the most illustrious of the families of San Antonio. The Señora, from the shaded depths of her own, watched their arrival. Nothing could be more characteristic than the approach of her daughters. Antonia and Lopez, stately and handsome, came slowly, their high-stepping horses chafing at the restraint. Luis and Isabel drove to their appointed place with a speed and clatter, accentuated by the jingling of the silver rings of the harness and the silver hanging buttons on the gay dress of the Mexican driver. But the occupants of both carriages appeared to be great favorites with the populace who thronged the Plaza, the windows, the flat roofs of the houses, and every available place for hearing and seeing.

The blue flag of Texas fluttered gayly over the lovely city. There was a salvo of cannon, and then, into the sunshine and into the sight of all stepped the man of his generation. The physical charm of Houston was at this time very great. His tall, dignified form attracted attention at once. His eyes penetrated the souls of all upon whom they fell. His lips were touched with fire, and his words thrilled and swayed men, as the wind sways the heavy heads in a field of ripe barley.

As he stretched out his arms to the people, he declared:

"Whatever State gave us birth, we have one native land and we have one flag!" Instantly from the grim, blood-stained walls of the fortress, the blessed Stars and Stripes flew out, and in a moment a thousand smaller

flags, from every high place, gave it salutation. Then
the thunder of cannon was answered by the thunder of
voices. Cannon may thunder and make no impression;
but the shout of humanity! It is a cry that cannot be
resisted. It sets the gates of feeling wide open. And it
was while men were in this mood that Houston said his
last words:

"I look in this glorious sunshine upon the bloody
walls of the Alamo. I remember Goliad. I carry my
memory back over the long struggle of thirty years. Do
you think the young, brave souls, fired with the love of
liberty, who fell in this long conflict have forgotten it?
No! No! No! Wherever in God's Eternity they are this
day, I believe they are permitted to know that Texas has
become part of their country, and rests forever under
the flag they loved. The shouting thousands, the booming cannon, that greeted this flag were not all the
sounds I heard! Far off, far off, yet louder than any
noise of earth, I heard from the dead years, and the
dead heroes of these years, the hurrahing of ghostly
voices and the clapping of unseen hands!"

"It was like Houston to call the dead to the triumph," said the doctor, as he stood with the Señora in
her room that afternoon. He was unbuttoning her
gloves, and her tears dropped down upon his hands.

"He is a man by himself, and none like him. I
thought that I should never forgive him for sparing the
life of that monster—Santa Anna. But today I forgive
him even that. I am so happy that I shall ask Holy
Maria to excuse me the feeling, for it is not good to
permit one's self to be too happy. It brings trouble. But

indeed, when I looked at Thomas, I thought how wisely he has married. It is seldom a mother can approve of her daughter-in-law; but Abbie has many excellencies— good manners, and a good heart, and a fortune which is quite respectable."

"And strong principles also, Maria. She will bring up her children to know right and wrong, and to do right."

"*That*, of course. Every good mother does that. I am sure it is a sight for the angels to see Isabel teaching her children their prayers. Did you observe also how great a favorite Luis is? He lifted his hat to this one and that one—it is certain that the next election will be in his hand."

"Perhaps—I wish Lopez would take more interest in politics."

"He is a dreamer."

"But, then, a very happy dreamer. Perhaps to dream well and pleasantly is to live a better life."

"Antonia is devoted to him. She has a blessed lot. Once I did not think she would be so fortunate."

"Lopez was prudent and patient."

"Prudent! Patient! It is a miracle to me! I assure you, they even talk together of young Señor Grant! It is satisfactory, but extremely strange."

"You had better sleep a little, Maria. General Houston is coming to dinner."

"That is understood. When I spoke last to him, I was a woman broken-hearted. Tonight I will thank him for all that he has done. Ah, Roberto! His words today went to my soul! I thought of my Juan—I wondered if he knew—if he saw—and heard—" she leaned her head upon her husband's breast, and he kissed away the sorrowful rain.

"He was God's greatest gift to us, Maria. Dearest, I love you for all the children you have given me; but most of all, for Juan."

THE END